Reading this book, I found m̶... Josephine in the way sh̶... her looks and demeano... special to me. I know it's... just think about everythin̶... ...always feel like crying because I will always understand the struggle of being who I want to be while everyone else is still against that. Also, if *Kissing Olivia Winchester* gets its well-deserved movie adaptation, I'm ready to watch it more than I should.
— Sabrina Torres, *Goodreads*

Kissing Olivia Winchester is exactly the book I felt like I was always missing growing up. There aren't many books with positive representation of queer women, so to have this book that makes me laugh, cry, and blush all in one chapter while providing representation queer women deserve is more than I could ask for. I fall in love with Olivia Winchester every single time I read this book!
— Adrienne Civetti

I love this book start to finish. The story isn't some cliché with a nerd crushing on a mean popular girl or something like that. The book has real emotions. It inspired me to write my own lesbian novel. So thank you, Athena Simone, for this incredible book. You're amazing.
— Ty Johnson

This book is amazing and so open. It shows things that are most often censored to the public. It's a book about a lesbian couple with no shame. It's more than the stereotypes and tells a story about the undeniably awkward time trying to figure some stuff out about yourself.
— Hannah Roberts

Honestly, I'm still reading this over and over again because of its wonderful characters and writing. I think this story is beautiful. I wish I could have something like this book happen to me. This is bliss.
— Jackie Devit, *Goodreads*

I absolutely fell in love with this book. Not only is the plot enticing but the writing style is beautiful. This book will put you in a trance, making it impossible to put down with lovable characters, great humor, and just the right amount of drama. A well balanced book concentrating on young love, figuring one's self out, trust, friendship, family issues and more. It will take you on an emotional roller coaster but one you will thoroughly enjoy all the way.
— Fizza Hasan, *Goodreads*

Typewriter Pub, an imprint of Blvnp Incorporated
A Nevada Corporation
1887 Whitney Mesa DR #2002
Henderson, NV 89014
www.typewriterpub.com/info@typewriterpub.com

ISBN: **978-1-68030-972-0**

DISCLAIMER
This book is a work of fiction. The characters, incidents, and dialogue are drawn from the author's imagination and are not to be construed as real. While references might be made to actual historical events or existing locations, the names, characters, places, and incidents are either products of the author's imagination or are used fictitiously, and any resemblance to actual persons living or dead, business establishments, events or locales is entirely coincidental.

KISSING OLIVIA WINCHESTER

ATHENA SIMONE

*To my family, friends, and Wattpad readers
who pushed me to keep moving forward*

FREE DOWNLOAD

Get these freebies and more when you sign up for the author's mailing list!

athena-simone.awesomeauthors.org

CHAPTER 1
The Kissing Booth

I wasn't here because I wanted to be. I was here because I was forced to be—forced by my monster of a mother, Melody Montgomery.

My mother was a part of the high-class country golf club. The men —who included my father, Hal—played golf in the club, boasting about the success of their businesses and their large sums of money while their wives drank tea, planned parties, and bragged about their oh-so-well put together sons and daughters.

The women raised money by holding a plethora of charity events to be able to fund the club without having to get a single penny from their pockets. It also gave them purpose.

Usually, my mother doesn't involve me in her schemes to show off to the other women. That's my sister Gwendolyn's job. I am not what you could call very social. I'm barely able to speak when it comes to people I am not very familiar with, so that leaves my sister to be the socialite of the family.

Since I turn into a stuttering idiot when people are around me, my mother brags about how amazing my sister is and takes her to the fancy get-together the club holds and leaves me at home.

Not that I'm complaining or anything. I'd rather read a book and be left alone anyways.

But this time, my mother just refused to leave me alone. She claimed it was life or death.

My mother's grand plan for fundraising this week was a carnival – with all the Ferris wheels, cheap roller coasters, greasy corn dogs, and creepy clowns that came with them. Every job was to be done by the children of the country club members, so they didn't have to pay for employees.

There was one job that wasn't taken by someone, most likely because it was the most unappealing position, even next to the person who cleans the leftover garbage. Since I was the only offspring left of every member of the country club, I was stuck working at the kissing booth.

I know, I know. It sounds like I'm over exaggerating, but I'm not. Not only is it embarrassing as hell, but it's also disgusting. Sure, you get to kiss a couple of cute guys here and there, but then come along the old geezers that probably haven't been kissed by anyone in years or the people that just don't know how to keep their saliva to themselves.

Oh, and if you're pretty, you're lucky enough to get a whole line of people just waiting to put their grimy lips against yours.

I'm fortunate because I was born with my mother's long flowing blonde locks and my dad's sea green eyes. Where I live as a natural blonde is like God's gift or something. I wasn't ugly or anything, quite the opposite. But my bright sea green eyes were usually hidden behind the lens of my glasses, the curves of my body covered by my baggy clothes, my hair was unkempt when I don't feel like brushing it through. I wasn't the type to get all dolled up.

And the worst part about the whole kissing booth ordeals was that I was forced out of the clothes I was comfortable in and stuffed into a square neckline knee-length white summer dress that flared out at the waist. The dress wasn't hideous, it just wasn't my thing. It made me feel incredibly awkward. And to put the cherry on top, I was obliged to wear pale yellow heels to go along with it. The curves of my body could be seen from a mile away.

2

To make sure my mother came out on top of making more money than the other women, she even tried to curl my hair. Luckily, my sister was having a hair crisis herself, so my mother just ran a comb through my hair to make it look presentable.

So here I was, sitting on an uncomfortable stool, with the hot sun beating down my neck in this tight ass dress. Nothing could make this better, and the carnival hadn't even started yet.

I sat there with nothing to do but rub my dry eyes due to the contacts my mother forced me to wear and stare back at the people who stared at me as they walked by. Apparently, no one recognized me, since I was in such an unusual attire. Well, for me that is.

"Josephine! Is that you?" I jumped in my seat at the loud shriek coming from behind me.

I turned to see Mrs. Ramsey, with a broad smile on her face and her son standing behind her. She had her arms open, waiting for a hug. I stood up and gave her a tight squeeze.

Susan Ramsey was the most down to earth, sweet as homemade cherry pie, mother in this whole entire country club. Others were at best stuck up and rude, but not Mrs. Ramsey. She was kind no matter what the circumstances were. Her exuberant personality and bright red hair attracted lots of attention like moths to a flame.

For some odd reason, a kind woman like her decided to latch on to my dysfunctional family when we first moved to Cranbrook when I was at the tender age of seven. She was always around to babysit me when my parents had more important things to do than take care of their own child.

I latched on to her just as much as she did to my family. She was my self-proclaimed godmother. Her husband was kind too—until Mrs. Ramsey found out that he was cheating with a co-worker of his.

Their divorce was a mess, but only because it was filled with false sympathy thrown at Mrs. Ramsey. The sympathizers themselves were only thinking about sleeping with newly-divorced Mr. Ramsey. Her son, Neal, handled the divorce surprisingly well.

Neal had become my best friend, since his mother was around most of the time. She was obligated to bring him along.

Neal wasn't so much of a pariah as I was in our little world; he was only an outsider to the children of the country club members. He was the smartest kid I had ever known, which made him pretty badass in my book. But to everyone else, not so much. Although Neal wasn't like any other nerds, he was very outspoken and at times, immature. He was still the guy that the lacrosse players pushed into lockers when they felt like it. He was the guy that the cheerleaders felt the need to ridicule just because he got good grades.

But to the parents, he was the guy they wanted their children to be, which only made kids hate him even more in return.

Since we were both outcasts in some way, we decided to stick together rather than to fend off the vicious high society alone. Now, at the age of seventeen, we only always had each other.

Mrs. Ramsey and Neal were the only two other people outside my family I felt remotely comfortable around.

"My, my. You look gorgeous, honey. Your mother did one heck of a job cleaning you up, hardly even recognized you!" Mrs. Ramsey exclaimed, giving me a once-over.

"I'll say." Neal snickered from behind his mother, clearly making fun of me. I knew he was fooling around because we were practically siblings. We didn't look at each other that way.

And if it weren't for the dress I was wearing, he would be screaming in pain right now. I just settled on glaring at him.

"Neal, be polite." Mrs. Ramsey chided her son.

He huffed before folding his arms across his chest, wrinkling his nicely-pressed pale blue button-up polo shirt.

"You look very pretty, Joey."

"Thank you, asshole," I retorted with an awkward grin, not used to the attention.

"Language. You look more than pretty, you look absolutely stunning. How about a twirl?" Mrs. Ramsey suggested, pointing with a circular motion.

I groaned, staying still. Mrs. Ramsey again twirled her finger. I knew my resistance was futile.

I turned very slowly, trying hard not to fall on my ass in these heels since we were standing on the grass. Mrs. Ramsey clapped excitedly.

"Wonderful. God knows your mother has been trying to put you in a dress for years. Speaking of your mother, let me go and find her to congratulate her on accomplishing such a feat."

She tapped me lightly on the shoulder and pointedly looked at Neal as if to say, *Stay out of trouble*, and then she walked off in the fray of people milling about trying to set up the carnival.

"You do look ever so lovely, darling," Neal said with a heavy country drawl.

Now that his mother was gone, I didn't have to be so polite. I punched him square in the shoulder.

"Ow!" Neal shouted, rubbing his shoulder. "That wasn't very ladylike now, was it?"

"I don't care if it was ladylike or not. I'll kick your scrawny ass if you don't shut it." I smirked, knowing it was true. Neal was almost darn near a pacifist.

"Fine, fine," Neal said, holding his hands up in mock surrender, then he bashfully put his hands in his khaki shorts. "How much did your father give you this time?"

My face hardened at his question. Usually, when my mother has some scheme to make me look presentable like my

5

sister and the other daughters in the club, and I resist, my father pulls me to the side and bribes me to make my mother happy. But what about making me happy? Nope, it's all about making sure my mother doesn't throw a hissy fit.

Don't get me wrong, I love my father. He was always there when he can be; he at least tried to understand who I was, unlike my mother who only wanted to make me into what she wanted.

"He gave me a fifty," I said, solemnly sitting back on the stool. I didn't like it when my father thought he had to bribe me to keep the peace, and fifty dollars weren't enough compensation for what I was about to endure.

"I'm sorry, I know how much you don't like when he does that," Neal said awkwardly, his right hand scratching his rusty orange hair.

"I'm over it." I'm really not, but I said it to appease him. "What are you still doing here? Don't you have a job of your own?"

"This is my job. Bodyguard at your service, ma'am!" Neal shouts straightening his body and saluting.

"What do I need a bodyguard for?"

"In case anyone tries to get handsy…if you know what I mean. No telling what those scoundrels will try to with you being all swanky and whatnot."

"What can you do, strangle them with your spaghetti arms?" I stated quizzically. Neal had yet to fill out like the other guys his age who had been through puberty. He had wide shoulders but was very scrawny. Neal was about 5'8", which was short for a guy, especially compared to the guys that went to our school. His arms had little to no muscle on them, which made him protect me laughable.

"I'll kick their asses. That's what!" He flexed his arms. I laughed at his antics, knowing he will probably get pummeled if he tried to start a fight with someone.

6

Sadly, my mother walked toward us as Neal cursed rather loudly. I clamped my mouth shut, sitting up straight knowing my mother will criticize my posture.

"Neal, you really need to improve your language. That is no way for a young man to speak," she said, putting her white Prada sunglasses through her sun-kissed blonde hair. She wore a floor-length robin's egg blue summer dress paired with white pumps. She looked elegant even though we were at a carnival. It was so nauseating.

"Sorry, Mrs. Montgomery," Neal said, hanging his head in shame. She turned her nose up at him as an acceptance of his apology.

"Now, I had Mrs. Ramsey put you two together because I know how Josephine feels about other people, but don't take my kindness for granted," she said with a disapproving glare.

"For Heaven's sakes!" My mother then exclaimed. "Josephine, would it kill you to sit up straighter? Ladies don't slouch. Have I not taught you anything?"

I tried to look like I was sitting up straight if it was possible.

"Good, now the carnival is starting. People should be lining up any minute now since you look…" she paused before giving me a once-over. "Somewhat…decent." Even after she dressed me, she still didn't approve of how I looked. I lowered my head in response, not wanting to make eye contact.

"I'll leave you two to your work." She flipped her hair over her shoulder, then turned to leave, but turned back to point at me "Don't embarrass me."

I nodded, not knowing what to say to her. I rarely had anything to say to my mother.

After she left, Neal looked at me with an apologetic smile. I smiled back, already forgetting about my mother.

"Oh! I forgot to give you something," Neal said before frantically digging in his pocket. He found what he was looking for and stuck it out toward me.

7

"What is it?" I asked before taking it, apprehensive. There was no telling what he was trying to give me.

A wicked grin broke out on Neal's face. "It's a ChapStick! I think you will need it." He was clutching his stomach now, shaking with laughter. My face heated up, embarrassed at the thought of how many people might line up to kiss me.

It is going to be a long day.

CHAPTER 2
Olivia Winchester

When I said it was going to be a long day, I wasn't joking. Apparently, my mother did an excellent job of making me look presentable because as soon as the carnival was open to the public, people of all ages came lining up in front of the booth.

I was also right when I said there would be old geezers and saliva geeks. But there were also tons of kids who went to my school that lined up to get a kiss from me. Surprisingly, no one recognized me, or just really didn't care. They were still just as eager when they made it to the booth, and if I'm not mistaken, I could have sworn some people got in line twice.

All the while, Neal stood beside me, grunting, trying to hold back his laughter. I had to refrain from punching him, knowing I would be in for a talking to if my mother found out I was being unladylike. Neal just stood there, laughing at my misfortune. He only had to pull this guy off me once, but that was only because the guy had too many beers.

Other than that, the whole ordeal went smoothly. Well, minus having to kiss a bunch of strangers.

As the sky grew darker, the line began to dwindle. Lucky for me, there were only about four or so people left.

"What are they doing?" I heard Neal murmur just as the next customer stepped up. The customer was just a little tike. His hair was gelled back nicely, and he wore a nice green button-down and brown pants. I held up a finger to him to signal that I needed a moment.

I turned to Neal. "What are you doing?" I asked curiously. Neal simply pointed to a group of girls standing off to the side of the small line. They were causing a bit of commotion, talking and joking around very loudly. It appears they were waiting for someone.

I shrugged, not thinking anything of it. "So, they're probably waiting for their boyfriends or something. Keeping an eye out so I don't get out of hand, most likely."

"They better be," Neal said, crossing his arms in defense. I knew he thought they might come here to pull some prank on the poor sap that got stuck with the job of the kissing booth. I was used to being ridiculed to the point where it didn't even bother me much anymore.

"It's fine," I said before focusing my attention back to the little boy in front of me. He was too short to even reach my face, let alone look over the booth. I stepped around the booth and bent down in front of the boy.

"Hi," I greeted, not knowing what I should say. I wasn't good with children either.

"Hi, you look pretty, lady," the little boy stated.

"Thanks. You want that kiss now?" He puckered his lips in response. I reached up to hold the left side of his face and kissed him on the cheek.

"Hey! That's not what I paid for!" He pouted.

"Sorry, kid, got to keep it PG," I said, cracking a small smile.

"This stinks!" the boy said before stomping off. I guess he really thought he was going to get a kiss on the lips.

"Man, I bet that wasn't the only heart you broke today," a soft voice spoke beside me. Still bent down, I stared upward. My eyes travel up from the pink sandals; smooth, creamy legs; a pink floral sundress to meet warm, honey brown eyes.

I quickly stood to stand eye level with the girl that had spoken. I gasped a little realizing she was closer than I had anticipated. The girl had long chocolate tresses that framed her pale but creamy face perfectly. As I looked into her eyes, I could see bright flecks of green. A dazzling smile was etched on her face. She was just breathtaking.

My eyes widened when I realized who was this girl standing in front of me. She was Olivia Winchester. She was the daughter of the wealthiest couple in the country club, Francine and Samuel Winchester. Olivia was popular and downright gorgeous, but humble, all at the same time. Olivia was the girl everyone wanted to be. Everyone wanted to be her friend. She was also a notorious heartbreaker who went through relationships like used tissues. And what made her more alluring was that she was bisexual.

Here in Cranbrook, being gay or lesbian was like the ultimate social suicide. Not because of religion—nope—but because of reputation. Being a homosexual was like a blemish on your face. Being gay was an imperfection. For these parents, being gay didn't lead to a beautiful family with a man and a woman with equally beautiful children. But what did they know? They also thought spending hours sipping tea and talking about the latest gossip was a useful way to spend their time.

But Olivia broke all the rules. When she came out to her parents, it spread like wildfire. The peculiar thing was that no one dared shun her like she was some leper. But when the eldest son of the Merricks—James—came out of his closet, they sent him off to his grandmothers. He hasn't been seen since then. Everyone chased after Olivia because she was so bold to be who she was. She was considered perfect, so no one would deny her that.

Olivia was the perfect student, daughter, and friend all rolled into one. And here she was, standing in front of me while I worked at the kissing booth.

Actually, I'm surprised I didn't faint.

"W-what are you doing here?" I stuttered out rather unattractively.

Her smile grew before she looked down at her feet shyly. "It was sort of a dare, I guess you could call it? My friends and I heard that there was some new beautiful blonde working at the kissing booth. We wanted to check it out," she said, looking at me through her long eyelashes. I blushed furiously; the way she called me beautiful was different.

"So, are you?"

"Am I-I what?" I asked before wringing my hands nervously.

"Are you new around here?"

"Um, no," I said, shifting from my left to my right foot. I quickly looked at Neal. His face showed that he was still tense about the whole situation. "I-I'm the Montgomerys' daughter."

She gasped before giving me a slow once-over. "Josephine?" she said, but it came out like a whisper. I hated my name but coming from her, it sounded almost beautiful.

I nodded, blush coating my face again, knowing she was deliberately checking me out. "My friends call me Joey."

Well, my one friend.

"Joey," she said as if tasting it on her tongue. Then Olivia stepped close to me. I didn't dare breathe. "So, do I get my kiss now?"

My eyes widened. I didn't know she would actually want a kiss from me. I thought she was here to check out the competition or whatever. My heart pounded so hard in my chest, I was positive she could hear it.

"Well, one of my friends already gave my five dollars to your thug over there." She pointed at Neal, who, instead of looking tensed, bashfully looked to the ground knowing Olivia's attention was on him. "I should at least get what I paid for, even if I do think five dollars is a little much for just one kiss."

I looked over at Neal to see what he thought. He just shrugged, not knowing what I should do either. Well, she did pay...

12

"Okay," I whispered. I kissed so many people today, I didn't think I would want another kiss in my life.

Olivia smiled before stepping even closer. I could feel her warm, minty breath on my face. She raised her hand to lightly grip my chin as she pulled me closer. My heart was pumping in my chest so inhumanly fast. My eyes flickered down to her lips as a pink tongue darted out, wetting them.

Ever so slowly, my eyes fluttered shut as her soft lips finally connected with mine. Olivia's lips were softer and sweeter than anyone's I had kissed all day. I was so lost in her kiss I didn't even notice Olivia's hands traveling from my hips to the small of my back, where she connected her hands, effectively pushing our bodies close together. Then I felt her tongue swipe my bottom lip.

I didn't know if I would have let her deepen the kiss or not, but I didn't get a chance to think about it before someone placed their hands on my shoulders to pull me back.

I stumbled back into Neal's chest, legs still feeling a little unstable.

"That's enough!" Neal growled. Olivia had a slightly dazed look on her face. Her eyes made contact with mine, swirling with surprise and something else I could not place.

She shook her head a little before a small smile appeared on her face again. "Down, boy. I was just getting my money's worth."

She threw a sultry wink my way before walking toward the crowd of girls. The girls squealed and patted Olivia on the back. Surprisingly, some glared at me with envy. Olivia sent a warm smile at me before leaving with her pack of friends.

My eyes followed her as she walked into the crowd of people. Neal stooped to my eye level and shook my shoulders to gain my attention.

"You okay?"

"I-I'm fine." *I think.* I shook my head, clearing it of the clutter Olivia left behind. The booth now stood empty.

13

"Where did the others go?"

"They left. I guess they got a little impatient. What was that?"

I looked at the spot where Olivia went. "I have no idea."

CHAPTER 3
Nose Bleeds and Locker Doors

Lately, I been, I been losing sleep
Dreaming about the things that we could be
But, baby, I been, I been prayin' hard
Said no more counting dollars
We'll be counting stars
Yeah, we'll be counting stars

The alarm on my cell phone blared Counting Stars by One Republic, waking me from my deep dreamless slumber. I had no intention of waking up at all, considering the long day I had yesterday. Also, I barely got any sleep at all because of the constant tingling still on my lips left over from Olivia's kiss. I didn't know what possessed her to kiss me. Maybe it was the outfit. Whatever it was, it left me feeling confused. I didn't know what I should feel. Should I be excited or angry?

I knew for one thing that I was too nervous to go to school today because of how people might react toward me reverting into my regular self or the kiss that Olivia had planted on me. Hopefully, it would all blow over unnoticed by others, and I could get the day without so much as a hitch.

I knew life wouldn't be so kind.

I threw my arm out to my white nightstand, successfully grabbing my cell phone to shut off the alarm, but I managed to knock my plain black-rimmed Ray-Ban glasses to the floor. I sighed heavily, not ready to use extra effort at seven in the morning. I stuck one foot out of the cover and bent down to grab my glasses. I pushed them up on the bridge of my nose before climbing out of bed. Climbing was clearly the wrong word because somehow, in between getting my glasses, I got tangled in my thick purple duvet. I crashed loudly to the floor, groaning in pain from the impact. I could tell that this was not going to be a good morning.

I stood up once again, going to my closet and grabbing the first thing I deemed fine for today. I went into my own private bathroom, brushed my teeth, and quickly changed. I came out with a baby blue shirt that said, *I'm not playing hard to get. I'm playing leave me the f**k alone*, paired with some beige baggy cargo pants. Today, I had some energy to run a comb through my bedhead.

I shoved my phone in my pocket and slung my Nikon D3100 digital camera around my neck. Photography was one thing I had always felt was mine. I felt comfortable with my photos. I felt like they were always constant. I started it a couple years ago when Neal and I were cleaning out the atrocious room of his. We found some old camera his father had given to him; Neal didn't want it, so I took it. I have been in love with photography ever since. Naturally, I bought a better, more efficient camera later though.

I exited my room and slowly walked, not wanting to trip and fall, down the large semi-spiral staircase leading into the foyer of the house. I slipped on some red Vans and put on my backpack, which I had already placed near the door. I was about to continue my way outside until I saw a hot pink large sticky note stuck to the door with an envelope attached.

The note said:

> *Your sister left for school already. Some of the kissing booth earnings.*
> *— Melody*

I had no clue why she didn't sign it *Mommy* or *Mom*. Any term of endearment would have been nice.

Leaving notes for me was a usual occurrence. My parents were usually never home, and when they were, I didn't see much of them. My father was busy with work all the time since he was a surgeon. My mother was a housewife, but she always kept herself busy with organizing charity events and hanging out with other country club members. The same goes for my sister. She was either always off with her bitchy friends or her guy of the week, or just holed up in her room. I could say though that I knew my sister and my father cared, they just didn't have time to show it. Sadly, I couldn't say the same for my mother.

I opened the envelope to find a mere forty bucks. After all the hard work I put into the stupid kissing booth, I had somehow earned close to two hundred bucks, and out of it, all I got was forty dollars. I bet she didn't even think of paying Neal.

I shook my head, not wanting to think about her any longer. I slipped the money in my pocket and crumpled up the Post-it and envelope and dropped them right where I stood just to irk my mother, knowing she liked her house spotless.

I went out of the house, locked the door, and walked to my white 2016 XTS Cadillac. Just because I was not shallow and spoiled didn't mean I didn't want nice things. My parents were loaded; why not buy what I wanted?

I hopped in, put the car in reverse, and slowly exited the driveway. I drove down a block or so before I stopped in front of Neal's house. I sometimes give Neal a lift to school when I was in the mood to put up with him. But I can't lie; I usually picked him up every day. I honked the horn loudly to let him know I was waiting outside.

Neal came racing out the front door with his hands full of papers and his backpack halfway on his shoulder. Some of the papers scattered, floating in the wind.

"Damn it!" Neal shouted before ambling around, trying to chase his papers before they blew away. I honked my horn again just to get on his nerves, knowing he was already frustrated. I laughed when he threw up the middle finger my way before going back to gather his mess.

When he was done, he rushed over and got in the car. Neal exhaled loudly before putting his papers neatly in a folder. "I was up late studying, so I sorta overslept."

I nodded before driving off towards our school.

At a red light, I pulled one of the twenties out of my pocket and stuck it out towards Neal.

"This is your pay for helping out at the kissing booth. I know it's not much since we made almost two hundred, but it's something." He took it with a smile.

"I wasn't expecting anything, so thanks."

I nodded before staring back at the road. The rest of the trip was relatively quiet until Neal decided he wanted to give the new One Republic CD I had just bought a listen. From then on, Neal shouted out the lyrics he had just learned very obnoxiously, not caring about the strange looks he was receiving from other people in their cars. I ducked my head, focusing on driving to hide my embarrassment.

When we had arrived at the school parking lot, I turned down the music, not wanting any more attention. As I grabbed all my stuff from the car, Neal crossed his arms and leaned on top of the car, looking at me.

"So, what are you going to do about..." He paused before looking around like he was saying something top secret. "You know who."

I gathered my stuff and began walking toward the school building. Cranbrook High had a wide parking lot in front of large stairs that halfway circled the building. Kids loitered on the stairs, not ready to start the school day yet. I didn't really blame them.

"You say it like Olivia's Voldemort or something," I stated while opening the door to the entrance of the school. I headed straight for my locker. Neal followed behind me since his locker was only a few rows down.

"I think she would fit more as a Dementor. Especially, how she was sucking your face yesterday," Neal said, wiggling his eyebrows at me. I gave him an uneasy smile, not comfortable with what he was implying.

"Maybe she was acting weird because she had a little too much to drink. You know how kids like to drink when adults aren't around." I lied, knowing I didn't taste any alcohol on her sweet strawberry-tasting lips. What was I just saying? I shouldn't care what flavor her lips were.

"Yeah, and I'm Hitler's cousin." Neal scoffed. A distraction came along when a hulking lacrosse player bumped me on the shoulder when he walked past.

"Hey! Watch it!" Neal shouted, always so keen to protect me. The guy turned and glared at Neal, which easily made him shrink back. With satisfaction, the lacrosse player went on his way.

"Close one," Neal mumbled. I nod. I thought I was going to have to go the rest of the day trying to find out the locker combo of the locker Neal had been shoved in. I grinned at him as a silent thank you.

We walked in a comfortable silence through the crowded, noisy hallway. Luckily, we didn't run into any more giant lacrosse players on our way over. When I made it to my locker, Neal continued to his.

I quickly twisted the locker dial to the correct combination; it popped open with one try. My locker was full of pictures, including a couple of my sister and me. Most were of Neal and me goofing off in some way. I admired the pictures before swiftly grabbing the books I needed for the first half of the school day knowing the bell was about to ring. I also took my camera off and set it inside because I wouldn't use it until lunch.

When I closed my locker, Neal was leaning against the lockers adjacent looking towards the ceiling. "I just don't get it. Why would Olivia kiss you after only getting in line to see who you were? Really, she could have just walked away after getting what she wanted. But no, she locked lips with you instead," Neal said, clueing me in on what he was thinking.

I sighed heavily. Why couldn't he let it go? I was ready to just forget about it completely. "I don't know either." I walked past him towards my first class. Neal didn't have a class with me, but he usually walked me to class, wanting to make sure no one bothered me on the way.

"It's very puzzling. Like I get that you looked really pretty." He grimaced, not wanting to think of me in that way. "Or whatever, but you're still you, right?"

"Look, I really just want to move on. Olivia probably already has, so why can't we?"

"I know, Joey. But it's just killing me, you know. Like could there be a possibility that Olivia…might like you?" Neal said in a sort of whisper. My head whipped towards him in shock.

"W-why would you think that? I mean, it was just one kiss," I said, my voice going up an octave with nervousness.

"I was just…"

"We haven't even had a full conversation. It would be impossible for her to like me. I'm just me, and she's all popular and stuff. I'm not even gay for crying out loud."

"Joey…"

"Just because she kissed me doesn't mean anything. It was a kissing booth. You're supposed to kiss people!" I continued ignoring Neal. *What if she does like me?* I didn't understand. It was impossible for her to. We didn't even know each other. I dressed differently just once, and now things are all confusing. But I couldn't figure out if I was more worried about a popular girl paying actual attention to me or the fact that I might have secretly liked the kiss. Just a little.

"Joey, watch it!" Neal shouted to get my attention. It worked because I finally looked away from him and looked in front of me, which was a mistake. Apparently, while I had been rambling and thinking about Olivia, I hadn't noticed that we had drifted closer to the rows of lockers. So, unfortunately, when I looked ahead, I slammed directly into someone's metal locker door.

The force of slam was enough to make me fall backward on my ass. My glasses flew somewhere in the middle of the door, hitting me and me falling. I groaned as a sharp pain traveled through my nose, ignoring the fact that my butt ached too. My hand flew to my nose to clutch it to try to ease the pain, though it only made it worse.

"Oh my God!" a voice shouted. I assumed it was my assailant. I couldn't look at their face. My eyes were tearing up from the pain, and my vision was blurred because I was blind as a bat without my glasses.

"Joey! Are you alright?" Neal shouted, kneeling down to the floor next to me. The other person stooped down as well.

"I'm so, so sorry. I didn't even see you there. Are you okay?" I didn't say anything. I just wiped my eyes so I could see who smacked the shit out of me. I gasped when I realized I had recognized that voice. I was looking in the face of none other than Olivia Winchester—well, what I could see of her anyways. Obviously, my plans of avoiding her all day have failed. Olivia and Neal gasped for different reasons.

"Oh God, you're bleeding, Joey. Like, I mean a lot," Neal said with a pitched voice. I looked at my hand and noticed it had an orange-red tint from the blood getting on it when it held my nose. I also looked down at my shirt, which was completely ruined now since it was slightly covered in blood. If the police saw me like this right now, they would most likely accuse me of murder.

21

"I am so sorry," Olivia repeated once again. "We need to get her to the nurse." Neal nodded, put his arm around my back, and slowly lifted me from the floor. I soon noticed that everyone in the hall was staring our way. I really didn't want the attention right now. It was already embarrassing enough to have gotten hit with a locker door, and Olivia's, no less.

"I got your glasses, but I can't put them back on because I don't know the condition of your nose," Neal told me as he shifted his arm around my back so that we were standing comfortably.

"Tilt your head ," Olivia said, putting her hand lightly on my chin to tilt my head. The gesture made me remember how she touched my chin before she kissed me, which only made my face glow more in embarrassment.

"I'm fine r-really. It's just a nosebleed," I said while getting out of Neal and Olivia's grasp. Without the support of Neal, I suddenly felt a little unstable. Olivia must have noticed my eyes drooping and my legs wobbling because she rushed back into my personal space and wrapped her arm around my waist.

"I don't think so. Neal and I will help you walk to the nurse's office." I couldn't look her in the eye, knowing how close we were and feeling how nice her arm settled around me. I pushed her arm off, not wanting to look weaker than I had already. I may have looked like an ax murderer with blood all over right now, but I still had some of my dignity.

"I can walk." I started turning towards the direction of the nurse's office. I didn't even make it a step before my vision blurred dangerously and I fell to the ground. The last thing I remembered was the same lean form before arms circled my body again.

CHAPTER FOUR
Pink Jackets

I woke with the feeling of delicate fingers as they caressed the side of my face lightly, tucking a strand of my blonde hair behind my ear.

I shifted my head, trying to lean into the touch.

My eyes cracked open slightly before I lifted a hand to rub my tired eyes. I finally opened my eyes fully only to see a beautiful, familiar face.

"Am I dead?" I asked, not believing the sight in front of me. The lights of the room shined behind the person leaning over me. Long brown hair reached down to tickle my cheeks. A glowing smile grew on the girl's face, clearly amused by my question. Her warm brown eyes stared at me matching her smile.

"No, you are not dead," Olivia responded softly. She backed away from me, giving me space. My eyes followed her involuntary.

"What happened?"

"To sum it all up in the best way that I can, I slammed my locker door in your face." Olivia looked at her sandals guiltily. "Which I am super sorry for by the way."

I sat up on the cot I was lying on and swung my legs over the side, with only a small amount of vertigo.

I ended up in the nurse's office. I could tell because everything was orderly and white. There were counters lined against the wall with cabinets above them full of different objects for sick people.

I wiped my eyes again trying to get out of my grogginess. I winced when my hand brushed against my nose. It pounded under the contact like it had its own heartbeat.

Olivia noticed my pain because she rushed over to the sink and grabbed an ice pack.

"Here," she said, coming to stand in between my legs. Olivia, once again, gently put her fingers under my chin to hold my head in place. She gingerly placed the ice pack on my nose.

My face heated up quickly, embarrassed that she was so close. The now familiar feeling of her breath on my face washed over me. My body couldn't help but react to her, even if I didn't want it to.

I let my eyes dart away from her face to look around the room. I realized Olivia and I were the only ones in the room. It only made my face burn even redder.

"W-where is Neal?" I squeaked out.

"Oh yeah, he went with Mrs. Hersh to get some supplies she couldn't carry herself. I am sorry, you know, about your nose."

"S-stop beating yourself up about it. I'm, uh, normally this clumsy," I say, still noticing her warm fingers under my chin.

"It was sort of like fate anyways, even if fate wanted me to hit you in the nose," Olivia said, lifting my chin a little to connect my eyes with hers. Thank God for the ice pack on the bridge of my nose or else Olivia would have seen how red my face really was. "I was looking for you."

"W-why were you looking for me?" My high-pitched voice clearly showed my nervousness.

"Because..." Olivia drawled out slowly with a bashful grin. She didn't get to finish her sentence because Mrs. Hersh came in with Neal trotting behind her. Olivia stepped back from me quickly but still stared at me with mischief in her eyes.

"Can I at least get one sucker?" Neal pleaded.

Mrs. Hersh glared at Neal. "No, I only give candy to my patients."

Neal went to the counter and dropped the box heavily. "But I helped carry the box; I should at least get something."

Mrs. Hersh just went on to ignore him and turned towards me. "How's your nose?"

I broke the staring contest I was having with Olivia. "It still hurts a little bit, I guess."

"Well, Mrs. Winchester managed to give you a nice little bruise on your nose there," Mrs. Hersh said, flicking a hand towards the direction of my nose. "The only thing you can do is ice it to reduce swelling and take some Ibuprofen to make it easier to deal with the pain."

Neal still looked miffed about not getting his candy, but he stared at me with concern. I just nodded to tell him that I was fine. His eyes flickered towards Olivia, eyebrows raised with questions. I just waved him off.

"Would you like me to notify your parents?"

"No." I shook my head glumly. "They won't care anyway," I mumbled. Mrs. Hersh had already turned away to unpack the box that Neal brought, so she didn't hear the last part, but Olivia did. Olivia's eyes bore into the side of my head while I sat there staring at my lap, refusing to look at her.

"Would you like some candy?" Mrs. Hersh interrupted.

I nodded my head eagerly. Candy was a thing that I loved, as well as Neal. I didn't even know why. But I would rather eat candy than eat everyday food. All types of candy were simply heaven.

Mrs. Hersh handed me a jar full of Dum Dum suckers of all flavors, then she turned back to finish restocking the cabinets. I hurriedly took a hand full of suckers and stuffed them in my pockets. I winked at Neal. He danced in his spot, excited about our "feast" later.

Olivia stood near me, looking back and forth between Neal and me, not understanding our excitement but smiling nonetheless.

"Since you insist not calling your parents, I signed off on you. Your friends here were instructed to look out for you for the rest of the day," Mrs. Hersh said, continuing her work. I hopped off the cot, and Olivia shot to my side holding my arm. My eyes widen at the contact.

"W-what..."

"You got to slow down. What if you faint again?"

I raised my eyebrows, not really understanding why she cared. "I'm fine."

Neal just chuckled. "Says the girl who bled profusely from her nose, then fainted!" Olivia glared at Neal, who put his hands up in surrender. "I'm just saying."

I laughed, walking ahead of the two out of the nurse's office. "I can take care of myself."

Neal and Olivia follow behind me. "But what if..."

I cut Olivia off. "Besides, you two should be in class." I point my finger accusingly.

"I carried you to the nurse's office. You're heavy as hell, if I might add." Neal pointed back while I rolled my eyes.

I look at Olivia, waiting for her excuse. She boldly stares back at me. "I wanted to make sure you were okay."

My eyes widened slightly. I didn't think she would be so forward with me. The insides of my stomach flipped in all different directions. Our mouths were agape. Olivia just sweetly smiled at us. I couldn't wrap my mind around the fact that she would care at all. We weren't friends. I understood her wanting to make sure I was okay, but after she realized I was, she could have left. But she didn't.

The silence was covered up when the bell rang, and chatter filled the halls. Still embarrassed from the incident earlier, I tucked my chin into my chest. That's when I noticed the big dry spot of blood on my chest. Great.

26

In an effort to cover the huge spot, I crossed my flimsy arms over my chest. Neal snickered because my arms clearly couldn't cover it.

"Here," Olivia said before unzipping her bright hot pink jacket. She held it out towards me. I shook my head, refusing. "Take it."

Eventually, I took it because self-consciousness took over. When I examined the jacket, I noticed it had a small girl flipping, doing gymnastics on the breast, and in large, black letters on the back was the word *Winchester.*

My cheeks reddened at the prospect of wearing something that was clearly labeled Olivia's. I just nodded in thanks, but I knew if I spoke, it would be a failure.

I put it on and zipped it up. It was baggy around my small frame since Olivia was much taller than me. The smell of mint and lilacs lingered on the jacket; it was a strange smell but oddly comforting. I couldn't help but smile a little.

A warm smile broke out over Olivia's face as she admired the jacket on me. "It looks good."

The bell rang loudly. Neal looked at me in fear. "We got to go!" We both had science together with Mr. Wafer. He was basically the old man that yells at you to get off his lawn or he would tell your parents. But instead of telling your parents, Mr. Wafer would give you a nice, pretty F.

I didn't have Mr. Wafer until the fourth period, so apparently, I was unconscious for three class periods.

I quickly nodded in agreement. I turned to leave when Olivia grabbed my wrist. Warmth spread through my arm quickly. I almost impulsively pulled Olivia closer to me.

I had no idea why by the way. I thought maybe it's because she smelled so good? I just wanted to sniff her. Whatever.

"Can I walk you to class?" Olivia blushed a little. I mean like honest to God she *blushed.* Olivia retracted her hand and coughed a little to cover up the awkwardness. "I mean can I walk with you to, you know, make sure you okay and stuff?"

My mouth fell open again. Here was Olivia standing in front of me acting nervous.

It's like Opposite Day.

She usually went about her business not even noticing me. Olivia's flock of friends were constantly hovering around her, but now they're nowhere in sight. Olivia was going out of her way to make sure I, the person no one noticed, was okay.

The day couldn't get any more confusing. And I hadn't even been to algebra yet.

Neal spoke before I could. Not that I would have been able to formulate a sentence anyways. "I got her, since we have class together. You don't need to miss another one of your classes either."

Olivia bit her pink bottom lip and sadly said, "Okay, that makes sense."

Olivia turned to hurry off to her class when she turned back to say. "I'll see you later, Joey." It came out more as a statement than a question. It took all my will power to not shiver at hearing my name come out her mouth. She gave me one last smile before taking off. I let out a sigh of relief, letting my tense shoulders sag. I didn't know how to feel or act around her.

Neal and I looked at each other, both still confused at what game Olivia was playing. Suddenly, she was hanging around me (and Neal).

Neal's mouth dropped in an 'O' shape like he had just figured something out.

"What?"

"I think Olivia really does have the hots for you!"

I blushed before punching him in the shoulder.

CHAPTER 5
Rapunzel Band-Aids

Like I had predicted, when Neal and I arrived at class, Mr. Wafer already had his angry face on before we even opened the door. We swiftly explained what had happened, using my nose as clear proof since it did have a bluish-purple tint to it. I ducked my chin in my chest, letting my hair fall in my face to cover my embarrassment from the rest of the class.

We made our way to our seats, which were next to each other. Neal nudged my shoulder before we sat down, trying to reassure me. I gave him a small smile. I grabbed a notebook out of my backpack, ripped a piece of paper out, and folded it in half. I began to write these words: *I'm okay.*

When Mr. Wafer turned his back to write on the board, I subtly passed the note to Neal.

Passing notes always helped pass the time; I never really paid attention during class. I was an average C student. I wasn't stupid or anything. I just didn't try. School had no point in my opinion since I had planned to become a photographer or a curator of my very own photo museum.

Neal passed the note back.

Just checking. I know how overwhelmed you can get. With, you know, Olivia and all.

I thought about what he said for a minute before replying. I still didn't know how I felt just yet. Could possibly Olivia really want to be friends with me? Or could this simply be just her trying to clean her guilty conscience? For all I knew, it could've been some sick plot created to embarrass me even further.

> —*I've reasoned that she's just going through some guilt trip or something. It will eventually pass.*
> —*If you think so*

We continued to pass notes for the rest of the class. When the bell rung, we gathered our stuff and went to the door.

At first, I thought I was just imagining things. But as I walked down the hall, I felt like literally everyone was staring.

All eyes were planted right on my back.

"Why is everyone staring?" I asked Neal quietly as if someone was listening to our conversation.

"Olivia's jacket."

My God, I had forgotten that I was wearing Olivia's jacket. It was bright pink, no less, which made it more noticeable. There was only one Winchester at our school, so it wasn't hard to figure out whose jacket I was wearing.

I had half a mind to take it off. I would have if it weren't for the large blood spot. I would have to endure the whispers and the stares.

I hunched over and crossed my arms, swiftly walking to my locker. Neal followed close behind me trying to cover my back, so the people who hadn't already seen wouldn't. It was useless since those who saw would just tell the people who didn't. But it was sweet.

I arrived at my locker, unlocking it. I grabbed my camera and a couple more books for the rest of the day. At lunch, students could eat outside, so I used that time for my camera. Cranbrook High had one of the best courtyards. It looked great in pictures.

As I closed my locker, I caught a glimpse of Olivia. She was standing down the hall, surrounded by tons of girls. The girls seemed to be talking with excitement at a mile a minute. Olivia just stood silently, listening.

She must have felt someone looking at her because she looked up and caught my eye. A small but noticeable small appeared on her face. My face flushed bright red. I tried to hide behind Neal so she couldn't see me any longer.

"Let's go if you want to get some good seats on the hill," Neal said, dangling his arm over my shoulder. I knew he did it purposely to cover the name on my back. I leaned into him accepting it.

If I didn't think of Neal as a big brother, he would be my first candidate for a boyfriend. He was always caring for me, making sure that I was okay. My mother urged me all the time to make a move with Neal. I still gag when I think about it.

I had realized that if we wanted to get outside to go to the hill, we would have to walk right pass Olivia and her groupies. As we passed the group of girls, they all seemed too quiet. Even though I wasn't looking directly at them, I could feel the heat of their stares. I refused to look at them, even Olivia.

When we finally passed, both Neal and I let out a sigh.

"I hope you're right about the whole 'it's going to pass' thing."

"Yeah, me too."

We arrived at the hill just in time to get some good spots.

In the Cranbrook courtyard, there was a stone picnic table. There was a large fountain center with all types of flowers circling it. The hill was the best part. The hill sat just behind it all, stretching far enough up to be able to overlook everything else. Everyone wanted to be able to sit on it.

We got a spot right in the middle. We weren't too far up, but we weren't too far down either. Neal laid down on his back, then stretched his long arms and legs. He put his hands behind his head and closed his eyes, enjoying the sun beating down on his skin.

"Want some suckers now, since we were too lazy to go get an actual lunch?" I asked, already pulling the candy out of my pocket, knowing the answer would not be no.

He silently nodded. I began to separate the Dum Dum suckers by the flavors we liked. Neal liked all the weird flavors like root beer, coconut, cream soda, and the other gross flavors. I liked all the normal ones.

After they were separated, I set Neal's pile of suckers on his stomach. He chuckled, causing the suckers to wobble.

I settled mine next to me and stuck a watermelon flavored one in my mouth.

I looked over the scenery below me before deciding what I wanted to photograph. I would just be random today, no set plan.

My photo subjects ranged from the fountain, random people, flowers, and Neal with candy on his belly.

I sighed contently, looking over my pictures in my camera. This was one of the best parts of being a photographer: being able to look at the moments you had been lucky enough to capture.

Neal sat up, looking around while twirling a sucker in his mouth. He perked up when he saw some kids play Frisbee.

"I'm going to go play," he said, sounding childlike. I nodded, acknowledging what he said.

After he left, I laid back in the spot he had once been in. I angled the camera towards the sky. I had captured some pictures with amazing light.

Suddenly, as I took pictures, a dark shadow came over me. I squinted through the lens trying to see if it was just my camera.

It wasn't. Through my lens, all I could see was Olivia's bright smiling face.

Seeing her scared me, thus causing me to drop my camera on my bruised nose.

"Oh my God," I exclaimed, sitting up quickly, holding my nose in pain.

Olivia kneeled quickly next to me. "Shit, I did it again, didn't I?"

"Yes, but I'm alright."

"I hope you're sure," Olivia said with concern written all over her face as she stared at my nose. I felt very self-conscious with her examining me.

"How did you know it was me up here?" She simply pointed to the jacket.

"I know my jacket," Olivia said, shrugging. "Do you mind if I sit with you?"

"N-no, not at all." Why the heck did she want to sit with me? She's got plenty for more exciting friends, I'm sure.

She settled next to me. When I say next to me, I mean, maybe a little bit too close for my comfort. I could smell the familiar smell that came with Olivia, mint and lilacs.

"People have been talking," Olivia started. "You know, about my jacket. I didn't mean to cause you any trouble. I just wanted to help."

I just sat there not really knowing what to say. I was unusually speechless around her. I wanted to say the right things; I just didn't know what the right things were.

"Want a sucker?" I blurted. I could feel Olivia shaking next to me. She was laughing now.

"Sure," she said through giggles. She shifted to lay on her side, smiling widely. "You're always so simple and straight to the point. I love that."

I blinked at her unbelievingly. I sat up and dug in my pocket and gave her one of my favorite flavors, cherry.

"Thanks. Do you normally eat a lot of candy?"

I just nodded. "I love it."

"I can see that. How do you manage to eat so much candy but still maintain your figure?" Olivia said with her gaze

33

traveling up my back, scanning my neck and face. I looked away quickly so she didn't see my constant blush.

I noticed Neal on the courtyard, waving and jumping up and down. I waved back and smiled.

"Can I ask you something?" Olivia spoke, drawing my attention away from Neal.

"Yes?"

Olivia frowned a little. "Is Neal your boyfriend?"

I barked out a loud laugh before covering it with a cough. I didn't want it to seem like I was laughing at her.

"No, that would be gross on so many levels." I pause to think of what I wanted to say next. "You know how people say they don't like someone 'cause they're like a brother? Well, Neal is my brother. Maybe not biologically, but a sibling, nonetheless."

Olivia stared at me in awe. "That was the most I have ever heard you talk yet."

"Why did you ask, you know, about me and Neal?"

"I don't know," Olivia said and just left it at that. I could hear the bells ringing in the distance in the school.

Olivia stood and dusted her clothes off. "I'll see you around." I waved, watching her as she walked steadily down the hill. She turned back and smiled again before going over to her friends sitting at a stone table.

I sighed inwardly. Olivia had so many friends. It just didn't add up why she wanted to be near me. I was the school antisocial, and she was Miss Popular. The complete opposite.

It will eventually pass. At least I hoped. I didn't want to get close to her—I mean like as friends, not together. I don't like girls just to be fooled in the end.

Neal came charging up the hill. When he got to me, he was winded.

"So—*huff*—what did—*huff*—Olivia want? *Huff.*"

"Nothing, she wanted to talk I guess," I said as I got up front the ground. I began to walk towards the school with Neal following behind me.

"Why?"

I stopped walking; I turned to stare at him. "You know, when it comes to Olivia, I never seem to have an answer."

~

The rest of the day went on without any more casualties, thankfully. I didn't have any chance meetings with Olivia either.

When I arrived home from school, I noticed Gwen's yellow 2016 Porsche in the driveway. I groaned, knowing I wasn't going to have the house to myself like I had originally thought.

I clambered out the car with my things, locking the door. As I walked into the house, I could hear classical music coming from the kitchen travel into the foyer. Gwendolyn was a classical music connoisseur and a closet chef. So when the music was being played, I knew Gwen was creating something delicious.

Her cooking expertise was one of her traits that I loved. I usually cooked for myself, but I was happy when I could eat Gwen's meals. I took my shoes and laid my backpack at the door.

I walked in the kitchen to see Gwen's head in the oven. Pots and pans were all jumbled on the stove doing different things. "Hey, Gwen."

"Hey, Jo." She was the only one that called me Jo; it made me feel like her little sister when she called me that. Like we were closer than we really were.

"What are you cooking?" I said, hopping on the marble island that stood in the middle of the kitchen. The island had two bars stools and a sink. All the counter tops were made of marble, and the cabinets were light brown. The house also contained a dining room, but my family rarely used it, since we never really ate at the same time. It was only used when guests came over or someone was feeling extra fancy.

"Nothing special, just garlic shrimp pasta with toasted French bread," Gwen said as she pulled out a tray of toasted bread out the oven.

"It's probably better than ramen noodles. That's for sure."

"Nothing is better than ramen." I smirked. She was right; ramen noodles were awesome.

Gwen set the tray on the counter before giving me her undivided attention. "How was your—" Gwen shrieked before finishing her sentence. "Oh my God, what happened to your nose?" she exclaimed before gripping my chin to examine it just like someone did earlier, but it wasn't as light and warm.

I yanked away. "It's nothing."

Gwen looked almost furious. "It's clearly something since it's turned purple. Did some bitch at school do this? I swear I'll kill them." I smiled widely. I liked it when Gwen was protective. It made me feel like Neal isn't the only who would defend me.

"I got hit with a locker door," I mumbled, knowing how stupid that sounded.

"Are you serious?" Gwen said with an incredulous and small smile on her face. I just nodded, knowing where this was going. Gwen's burst of laughter caused my face to paint a bright red. "That is the funniest thing I have ever heard. You really must be more careful. Let me see if I can find something to reduce the swelling," Gwen said, walking over to the hall bathroom.

I sat and waited, still on the counter for her to come back. When she did, she held a wet folded paper towel and two Band-Aids. "I couldn't find a cold compress small enough for your nose, so I improvised. Which Band-Aid do you want? Toy Story or Rapunzel?"

"Definitely Rapunzel."

36

"Rapunzel, it is." Gwen placed the paper towel over my nose, then the Band-Aid on top to make it stick. "Now I'm going to finish cooking. You stay out of trouble." Gwen went back to the stove to continue her work, humming the classical song that was playing now.

I hopped off the counter. I was going to leave, but I had to take a couple pictures of Gwen cooking first. I snapped the ones I wanted before leaving.

Just as I reached the stairs to head to my room, the doorbell rang. I slid (my socks made it slippery) on the hardwood floor over to the door. I threw it open without even looking through the peephole. My mouth fell open as I stared at Olivia standing on my porch.

There I was with my mouth wide open and a Rapunzel Band-Aid taped to my nose.

CHAPTER 6
Interrogation and Flirtations

"Hi," Olivia greeted with a large smile on her face. I waved awkwardly. "W-what are you doing here?"

Olivia apparently took that as her invitation because she stepped up and walked right past me into my house.

Olivia Winchester was in my house. This could not get any weirder. All I could do was shut the door behind her.

"I just wanted to see you."

"N-no, really. What do you want?" It came out harsher than I had expected, but it didn't faze Olivia. She continued examining my foyer, poking her head into the living room. When she was done, she turned back toward me. A suggestive and amused smile crept up on her full lips. She walked closer and closer until our bodies were almost touching.

"I really did come to see you." Olivia reached up and touched the bridge of my nose, tracing the Band-Aid. I really had forgotten about the Band-Aid now that Olivia was being all...I don't know what to even call it. My brain was a mess. She was standing very close, and it was affecting me. "Seeing you in this super cute Band-Aid was such a bonus." Olivia chuckled. I could nearly feel each breath she took.

"Who is at the door?" Gwen shouted from the kitchen. Her voice broke the spell I was under. I stepped back quickly from Olivia, trying to put some distance between us, only succeeding in running into a tall floor lamp we had standing in the foyer. The lamp crashed to the floor, breaking the glass lampshade and the bulb inside. Glass shards shattered all over.

"Josephine!" I cringed, knowing I was in for it. This was literally the second item in the house that I had broken this month: first, the flower vase and now, this.

Olivia put her hand over her mouth to stifle her giggles. "Wow. You really are clumsy."

My sister stormed into the foyer to inspect what had been broken this time. "I told you to stay out of trouble, and here you go breaking things." She hadn't even noticed Olivia yet; she was too focused on the mess I had made.

"Let's hope Mom doesn't notice, which is not likely."

Gwen stopped her rant when she heard Olivia giggle again. She was laughing at my reaction this time.

"Olivia, what are you doing here? Are you here to see my mother? Because she's not in." She's never here.

The attention was off me now, so I tried to move and make my way up the stairs to go to my room like I had originally planned.

Gwen spotted my movement, pointing a finger at me. "Don't you dare move. Knowing you, you will probably end up severing your entire foot trying to get around this glass." I did as I was told and stood still.

Olivia, finally, was able to answer my sister's questions and said, "No, I actually came to see Joey. I, uh, hit her in the nose."

Gwen burst with laughter again at my expense. She couldn't say anything since she was laughing so hard. She wiped her tears when she calmed down. I stood there, blushing in embarrassment. "I'm sorry. That is just too good. I have never heard that actually happen to someone before."

Olivia smiled in agreement. "I think your sister is the first."

"Right you are. She is doing fine now though." Olivia didn't take her word for it because she looked toward me.

"I'm fine."

"I just feel responsible." Well, she kind of was responsible. "I guess I'll be leaving now…"

"How about you stay for dinner?" Gwen piped up. I could have slapped her for that.

"Thank you, but no, thank you. I only stopped by because I was on my way to my sister's middle school."

"Shame. Maybe next time." Like there will be a next time.

"Not likely," I mumbled. Thankfully, no one heard me.

"Maybe." Olivia glanced my way before exiting. "See ya," she said over her shoulder.

"Since when were you and Olivia friends? Better yet, when did you get friends besides Neal?" Gwen asked when we were alone.

"Why does everyone feel the need to ask me?"

"It's a valid question. Another valid question is why are you wearing Olivia's jacket?"

I simply went up the stairs, leaving my sister. "Tell me when dinner's ready."

~

As I shut my locker, Neal spoke up, "So I heard Olivia stopped by yesterday."

"Where did you hear that from?"

"Your sister," Neal said bashfully, running his hand through his flaming red hair.

"Since when did you have casual conversations with my sister? She's a senior—a year ahead of us—so it's not like you have a class with her." I stared at him quizzically.

"Um, I called yesterday while you were in the shower. And she told me then."

His answer seemed a little sketchy, but it was possible, so I shrugged it off.

The day was going by slowly but surely. Surprisingly, I have had a chance meeting with Olivia yet. I won't speak too soon; I might jinx it.

40

"I'll see you later. I have study hall."

"Alright, see you whenever. If you're not too busy with Olivia, that is," Neal said with a large Cheshire grin, wiggling his eyebrows.

I shoved him away from me. "Olivia and I don't hang out. I barely know her. We're not friends." Other than the fact that she was the most beautiful girl I had ever seen—I mean, like, everyone knew that—I didn't know much about her.

"From the looks of it, Olivia wants to be more than friends, if you know what I mean," Neal said, nudging me repeatedly in the arm. I shoved him away again.

"I'm leaving."

As I walked away from Neal, I heard him shout, "Tell Olivia I said hi!" I'm sure the people in Tokyo heard him. The people in the hall sure did. They all turned my way, giving me curious looks.

I ducked my head and walked briskly to the library, where I decided to spend my study hour.

I entered the library, scoping it out for a good spot. The library had large windows that made the area look bright, instead of dreary and sad. It was a friendly environment, which allowed students to talk and hang out. Of course, there were books stacked in rows of shelves. There were also pod chairs and beanbag chairs everywhere in random places.

I think it was supposed to encourage studying. Like we give you nice stuff, you learn more.

I went over and camped out at one of the tables near a window.

I spread out the books I needed so I can get some studying in. I had a test coming up that I could not really afford to fail. My C average would go way down if I did.

I pulled out my last sucker from my pocket, knowing I would need some sugar to get through this.

I soon got distracted when I started to feel like someone was staring at me. I lifted my head from my books to

41

look around the room. There were kids sitting in the pods, beanbag chairs, and some of the shelves but no one was looking at me.

When I turned back to bury my head in my books, there were three girls standing there who weren't there before.

I yelped in surprise, causing my sucker to fall out my mouth and onto the floor. I gazed at the sucker with sadness, mourning the fact that it was my last. I scooped it up off the floor, staring at it with grief. I wrapped it back up to throw away later.

I leveled my gaze at the three girls. Whatever they had to say better be damn important because it just cost me my last sucker.

They stood there unfazed, coolly staring back.

"You're Josephine?" the one in the middle with strawberry blonde colored bob said.

"Joey," I said curtly, still raging inside about my fallen sucker.

The one on the left—well, my left anyways—arched a fine eyebrow leering at my face. "She's not even that pretty," she said, flipping her light brown hair over one shoulder, looking away from me, uninterested.

"I think she does alright, you know, considering the clothes she's wearing," the girl on the right commented, looking at me up and down. Her gaze was more admiring than criticizing. She tucked her shoulder-length dark locks behind her ear as if to get a better look at me.

"Remember, she looks way different in other clothes."

"I'm literally right here," I interjected.

They went on to ignore me.

"Oh yeah, she didn't have those glasses either at the carnival," Lefty said, pointing to my glasses. I adjusted my frames feeling self-conscious under their scrutiny.

"From where I was standing, she still wasn't as pretty as Olivia described her," Righty said. The one in the middle stood silently, examining me. Olivia was telling people about me?

Then it just clicked. These girls were a part of Olivia's entourage. They were Jocelyn Bradford, Cassidy Summerfield, and Danika Vasquez.

These three reminded me of the plastics from the film *Mean Girls*. They were rich, superficial, and had a model-like beauty. The whole package.

They constantly were following behind Olivia, awaiting her every move. It was like they took a class called *How to be a Groupie 101* and aced it with flying colors. Hell, they taught the freaking class.

It was scary how much they wanted to be at Olivia's beck and call.

It was also scary how they were staring at me right now; two critical and the other, if I'm not mistaken, suggestive.

"What does Olivia even want with you?" Cassidy asked, squinting her eyes, finally adding me to their conversation.

"H-how am I-I supposed to know. You're h-her friends," I said, trying not to stutter. I wasn't comfortable around people I didn't know.

"What's with the stutter?" Jocelyn snapped. I didn't bother speaking to her.

"Whatever. She's not worth our time." Cassidy glared at me one last time before walking off with Jocelyn behind her.

I was going to go back to studying when I noticed Danika was still standing in front of me. She just stared at me.

"W-what?" I growled, trying to sound angry with a stutter. I wasn't in the mood to be played with.

"Your glasses don't look all bad," Danika spoke up. I gaped at her, dumbfounded. What? Honestly, this was the first conversation I have ever had with her, and she tells me my glasses don't look all bad.

"Okay..." I drawled out, still confused.

Danika smiled a little before giving me a wink (or maybe I thought it was a wink, but it was really a twitch) and taking her leave.

People are very strange.

It bothered me that people started to notice that Olivia hung around me more. I was not used to all this attention. I flew under the radar, so people didn't notice me. I like it that way. Now, everything was changing. All because I kissed Olivia.

I just had to stick with my mantra: It will pass.

~

When I got home from school, I was exhausted mentally and physically. Mentally because of school, obviously, and thinking about my confrontation with the brat pack; also Olivia. Physically because I was lazy, and school took a lot of effort.

I hadn't seen any of my family member's cars outside, so I assumed I was home alone. I slipped off my shoes as usual and then trudged up the half-spiral stairs. I entered my room, tossing my backpack on the floor.

My room was simple and comforting. I had a full-sized bed with a big fluffy purple duvet over it with purple pillows and such. The bed was paired with two mahogany end tables. I had an antique mahogany desk sitting on a wall in my room. My wall was painted orange. I know it was an odd color to go with purple, but I liked it. You could barely see the walls, though, since most areas were either covered by picture frames with my photos in them or bulletin boards with photos tacked on them. My room was my sanctuary.

I flopped on my bed, closing my eyes to take a quick nap before I did my homework, but I heard heels clicking on my hardwood floor. I opened one eye to be able to examine the intruder. It was my mother.

My mother looked as regal as ever. She wore a waist-high cream skirt with a slick peach button-up and white peep-toe pumps. She looked like she was going on some business trip when she was really going to gossip.

"What?" I groaned.

"Get up," my mother said curtly, walking to my desk to lean against it.

Without protest, I got up from my bed, standing awkwardly. My mother flicked a blonde curl from her face while she examined me.

"I rearranged your closet," she said shortly. Mother always spoke in short sentences when talking to me. It was like since I was her daughter, she felt obligated to communicate in some way.

I knew her definition of rearranged and mine were completely different things. I raced over to my walk-in closet. I opened the door, not knowing what to expect. My mouth gaped open at my new and improved wardrobe.

My regular comfortable tee shirts and jeans were no longer hanging in my closet. Dresses, slacks, button-ups, and different types of boo-styled clothes replaced them. Skirts and cute cut shorts were everywhere. All my Vans, sneakers, and Converse were gone. In its place were sandals and heels. I was completely appalled.

"W-what have you done?"

"I gave you a sense of style." My mother sneered, not happy with my response.

"Where are all my clothes? Why are they not here?" I still could not believe she replaced all my clothes, and without my permission. I was beyond furious. I barely saw her, and when I did, she thought she could just change things when she was never here.

At least Olivia's jacket was in my desk drawer so she couldn't take that. (I was only worried about it because I had to take it to the cleaners so I could give it back.)

"I changed your wardrobe so you can look presentable when your grandmother comes to visit. You will get them back

45

as soon as she leaves. I assume she won't stay for long," my mother said nonchalantly as if the entire situation did not matter. She gave me a curt nod before leaving me gaping in the middle of the closet.

It wasn't my grandmother Helen I was upset about; it was the clothes. I loved my grandmother probably even more than my own mother. She was one of the people who accepted me for who I was and didn't try to change me. My mother wanted to impress grandmother with her high status, but grandmother didn't give a rat's ass. So all my mother's efforts were in vain anyway.

I had to wear these clothes for the rest of the week. I thought I knew what embarrassment was before, but this showed me all the stuff I had been through wouldn't even compare.

I was pretty sure this week couldn't get any better. If you didn't catch my sarcasm, I'll spell it out for you: I'm screwed.

CHAPTER 7
Hermits Can Be Attractive

I stood in front of my full-length mirror in my bathroom, staring at the clothes I was forced to put on. I had no other choice but to either put on the clothes my mother bought or go naked.

I liked the first one much better.

This morning, my sister woke me up, storming into my room and going through my closet to pick an outfit for me, under my mother's order. She knew I would either not go to school or pick something hideous, so she had Gwen make sure I looked acceptable.

Gwen picked out a simple light blue chambray dress with white polka dots and buttons down the center. It was sort of tight fitting, so all my curves were on display just like my mother liked it. The dress didn't even reach my knees. Like whatever happened to dresses like that. The dress was luckily paired with white multi-strap sandals.

Gwen even pulled all my long hair blonde hair to one side, leaving some hair hanging on the other side and braided in a messy fishtail.

To top my morning off, my mother had the nerve to steal my glasses. When I went to reach for them on my nightstand, I found a box of contacts with a note saying, *You will get your specs back later.*

I really didn't want to go to school today.

I sighed begrudgingly. I went over to pick up the tote bag my sister happily gave me because apparently, you weren't supposed to wear backpacks with dresses.

I trudged down the stairs, trying to prolong my trek to school. Might as well get breakfast too, since I was trying to procrastinate.

When I walked into the kitchen, Gwen was at the bar, eating an apple and drinking a cup of coffee. I took the liberty of pouring some for myself.

I slowly took a sip, relishing in the dark liquid.

"Oh la la, don't we look fancy," Gwen spoke upon noticing me. She admired her handy work with a smile.

I slouched into the counter I was leaning on, trying to shy away from her stare.

"What did mother say about slouching? It messes up your posture," Gwen nagged teasingly.

"Blah blah blah," I mumble in the rim of the coffee cup.

"Okay, when you end up looking like a hermit, don't come crying to me."

"What if my life goal is to be a hermit, then what?"

She glared at me, not finding what I said funny. "You will be one attractive hermit then," she said dryly. "Neal called and said you don't have to pick him up this morning."

I groaned out loud. Great, now I would have to get to my locker without the protection of Neal. Everyone would see how I looked.

"Okay then," I said preparing to leave for school. Gwen stopped me before I could make it to the door. She unbuttoned the first button on the dress.

"For that extra…" Gwen said with a French accent. "Je ne sais quoi."

"Whatever. I'll see you later," I responded, not bothering to button it back up.

"Bye. Make sure your home on time for grandma."

"Whatever," I said, walking toward the front door.

Let's get the torture over with.

~

On the way to the school, I texted Neal to meet me at the school doors. I didn't want to have to walk all the way to my locker unguarded.

I pulled into the parking lot with a bundle of nerves. It was one thing to have to wear this kind of *revealing* clothes at the carnival. At school, it was a whole different thing.

At the carnival, teens were being watched by the adults, so they had to act a certain way. At school, you could act however you wanted. No telling how people would react to me.

I took a couple of breaths before exiting the car. I scoped out the parking lot. There were not many people hanging about in the area, and those who were weren't paying attention to me.

I grabbed my stuff quickly and made my way over to Neal.

Neal was leaning on a wall near the doorway, playing what it looked like an app on his iPhone.

I cleared my throat to get his attention. He pocketed his phone quickly. Neal gave me one glance before his features morphed with amusement.

"Oh my God," he said with an under-toning chuckle.

"Don't even."

"But...Why?" Neal grimaced, trying to hold in a laugh.

"My mother made me. Grandma is flying in, and she wanted to show off."

Neal suddenly stopped laughing. He patted my shoulder in understanding. "I'm sorry. Your mother is such an ass," Neal said in an attempt to make it better.

I smiled a little at that. "She's more of a bitch."

"How long do you have to wear this stuff?"

"Till my grandma leaves."

49

"Brutal. You look beautiful though, and if anyone says otherwise, I'll kick their asses," Neal said, puffing out his chest, trying to look muscular.

"Thanks."

"You ready?"

"Ready as I'll ever be."

Neal opened the door for me as we walked into the school. I ducked my head, preparing for the whispers and the stares.

As predicted, everyone's attention gravitated toward me. Some just stared. I even heard someone whistle. Others whispered comments like "Who's the new girl?"

That kind of angered me a little. I knew I looked a little different, but come on, I have lived in Cranbrook since I was little.

I just had to suck it up and keep moving forward. And that's what I did. Neal hovered close to me.

Finally, I reached my locker. Neal stayed with me, probably already having gone to his.

"Do hermit people have hunchbacks?" I rattled off randomly, trying to distract myself from the stares coming from all around.

"What? How am I supposed to know?" Neal snorted.

I shrugged, opening my locker. When the door opened, a plastic gift bag tied with a pink bow fell out and onto the floor.

I bent carefully as I could in a dress and scooped up the bag. There was a note attached that said:

I heard you dropped your candy
– O

My first thought was: How did some creep get into my locker? Then I realized it must have been from Olivia. At least that's what I thought. It could be from quarterback Owen Ashford, but I highly doubt that.

50

I didn't want to admit it, but I wanted it to be from Olivia.

I smiled softly at the bag, examining its contents through the clear container. There were, of course, my favorite flavors of Dum Dum suckers. But there were also some of my favorite candies. It held Hershey kisses, gummy bears, and sour Skittles.

How did Olivia know about my favorite candies? If I didn't find the gesture so adorable and my heart wasn't beating so fast, I probably would have thought it was creepy that she had gotten into my locker and knew my favorites.

Neal peeked out from behind my shoulder to get a look at what I was holding. He let out an excited squeal when he saw that it was candy. "Ohhh, can I have some?"

"N-no," I said, clutching the bag to me. Neal cocked his head to the side with confusion.

"Why not? You always share with me."

I didn't want to share this with him. This candy was meant for me and only me. Olivia intended for me to eat it, so I will. Look at me, getting all possessive over some candy.

"I-I don't want to s-share this time," I said with a small voice. I quickly put the candy in my tote bag, hoping he would just drop it.

Neal frowned, eyeing me with suspicion. "Who is it from?"

"I-I don't know. There was no-no note." I tried to lie smoothly, but my cursed stutter was getting in the way.

Neal huffed and crossed his arms. "Fine, don't tell me. I have a feeling I know who it is from anyways. But I'm not going to say anything."

Inwardly, I sighed with relief. I was glad he let it go and didn't bring up his notion. I wasn't ready to confront these strange feelings I was having about Olivia that I shouldn't. For now, I would just enjoy the candy Olivia had given me.

~

My classes went by rather quickly, considering I had to sit through each of them, enduring the stares, counting the minutes until I could dash out the classroom.

I hadn't seen Olivia all day. I hated to admit; I was constantly searching the halls for her luscious brown locks, trying to catch a glimpse of her somewhere to, you know, thank her.

I gathered my stuff ready to get to my locker. As I walked, I could feel a presence hover near me. I knew it wasn't Neal because his last class was on the other side of the school. I looked to my left, searching. No one was there, so I turned to my right.

Danika stood there smiling at me. I wasn't expecting her to be so close. So being me, I dropped the books I was holding in my hands.

I stooped to pick them, keeping my head low to hide my reddening cheeks. I can be such a klutz.

Danika stooped next to me to help me gather my books. People lingered around trying to see the commotion, but most moved on. "This is the second time I have scared you." She chuckled.

I stayed silent because of my nervousness and not knowing what to say.

"Strong, silent type, I suppose," Danika said, grabbing the last book, standing at full height. I stood as well, sticking my hand out, asking for my books.

She simply copied my gesture. "I'll carry them. Don't want you dropping them again." When I didn't hand them over, she smiled a bright smile trying to coax me. I reluctantly handed them to her.

"Lead the way."

I did, walking ahead of her. She followed behind me quietly. The reason I knew she was still there was that I could feel her gaze on my back and, do I dare say it, my backside. I'm not even remotely joking.

52

When my locker came into view, I could see someone leaning against the one next to it. I couldn't get a clear view of their face because they were staring down at their shoes.

Just as we were near, Olivia picked up her head to look at me. As her glance left my eyes, her jaw slackened, and her eyes widened just a little. Her eyes traveled up and down my body repeatedly. A shiver shot up my spine. I even gave a little smile.

Olivia cleared her throat, standing up straight. "W-why…your… clothes…umm, different," she said in fragments. I smiled even more because it was kind of adorable. I knew what she said though.

"My mother made me."

"Doesn't she look ravishing?" Danika spoke up now with a British accent, but you could tell she was serious about her thinking I looked *ravishing*. I had forgotten she was there.

Olivia turned her attention to Danika. Her gaze was no longer light and warm but cold and steely. Her grin vanished as she looked at Danika. Danika just stared back with a wickedly sweet smile.

"Danika."

"Olivia."

I watched as they stared at each other in some type of battle that I didn't know about.

"What do you want?"

"Joey…" Danika started but smirked with Olivia's jaw clenched at my nickname. "Had dropped her books, and I was polite enough to help her carry them back to her locker."

Olivia just glared, trying to find a flaw in Danika's explanation. "Okay. So, what are you still doing here?"

Danika's smirk grew wider. "Maybe I wanted to get to know Joey, seeing that we have gone to the same school for two years. And she doesn't seem to have anyone attached to her, so I thought why not." She made the word *attached* sound like it had a double meaning. Olivia must have caught it too because she raised a fine eyebrow.

"I think she can handle her own books now. So, you can just run along," Olivia said with a slight sneer, waving her hand in a shoo motion. Olivia's gesture causes a wolfish grin to appear on Danika's face.

"Okay, I'll leave." Danika swiveled toward me, resting a hand on my bare arm, handing my books back to me. "I'll see you later." She ran her hand lightly down my arm before parting.

Olivia glared at her with a scowl. I thought nothing of Danika after she left, only focusing on Olivia's facial expressions. She looked angry, but to me, it was just cute. For an odd reason these days, I found most things Olivia did cute.

I shook my head because I should not have been thinking that Olivia was cute, especially since she was standing right there. I went on to open my locker and shoved my books in and grabbed the ones I might need tonight. Olivia's eyes followed my every move as she leaned against the locker adjacent.

My motions slowed for a moment as I thought about the candy in my tote bag. "Thank you," I blurted, not looking Olivia in the face. "F-for the candy," I said in a whisper while blushing.

I could see Olivia's warm smile bloom on her face. "You're welcome. I wanted to do something for you since your other candy fell to the floor. I know how much you love it." Butterflies swarmed in my stomach at the fact she was listening and remembered a small thing like that about me.

"H-how did you even get into my locker? Or know my favorite candies?" I asked.

Olivia tried to look aloof but failed since she was smiling widely. "I have people."

"B-by people, do you mean Neal?" I had a hunch she got the information from him because he knew everything about me. Or it could have been Gwen.

"You will never know." She looked at me playfully smiling. I couldn't help but smile back. Olivia had one of those infectious smiles.

Maybe, just maybe, I didn't want this whole Olivia-hanging-around thing to pass. No, not just yet.

CHAPTER 8
Guess Who's Coming to Dinner

I pulled into my driveway with a giddy smile playing on my face. My heart rate was still racing from my meeting with Olivia. I didn't know what it was about her that made me...just feel. I could still feel the heat of her gaze on my skin as she stared at my unusual clothes. It made me feel like someone paid me some attention; I wasn't completely invisible.

I reached over the console to grab my tote bag when I noticed the bag of candy. My smile grew wider when I saw it. As I grabbed the rest of my belongings, I tried to wipe the smile off my face before I went into the house, since parked outside were both my mother's and my father's cars.

I walked into the house and slipped off my shoes immediately, no longer being able to stand wearing sandals. They have no support whatsoever. I might as well walk around barefoot.

I couldn't wait to eat the candies Olivia gave me. I would try to savor it, but I knew that wouldn't happen. I devoured any candy I found, so savoring it was a no-go.

"What are you smiling about, kangaroo?" a voice spoke. Once again, I got startled by an unexpected person. My grandma was leaning on the doorway leading into the kitchen. A smile was on her face. Her hazel eyes, identical to Gwen's, sparkled with amusement. Her hair had more gray streaks in it than the last time I had seen her, but she still looked young for sixty-five.

"Hi, Grandma," I said warmly and walked over to hug her. I had missed my grandmother. She, unlike my other family members, didn't try to change who I was. Oh, and bonus, she didn't ignore me like her daughter did because she thought I was like a "dishonor" to the family.

"Good Lord, what has she done to my little kangaroo this time?" my grandmother said disapprovingly. Grandma had always called me "kangaroo" as a nickname since we didn't like the name Josephine. A kangaroo's baby is also called a joey, so it fit.

I pouted, trying to look innocent. "I'm being tortured, Grandma."

"Yes, kangaroo, I know. But I can't do anything about that because she is your mother no matter how neglectful she is."

"You're her mother, though. Can't you, like, I don't know, put her in a corner or something?" I said, throwing my hands in the air playfully.

"I can't put her in a corner. She is way too old," my grandmother said with a hearty chuckle.

I leaned in close to her and cupped my mouth with my hands like I was telling her a secret. "And don't I know it. I'm pretty sure she is like in her fifties but hides it well under her makeup."

Grandma placed her arm around my shoulder, pulling me into a half hug. "I sure have missed you."

"Me too, Grandma." I could hear my father's laugh coming from the kitchen. I immediately let go of my grandma and jogged into the kitchen right into my father's side. He put a muscular arm around my back. My father, Hal, smelled like clinical supplies, Lysol, and Old Spice. It was a strange smell, but it was familiar.

"Hey, sweetheart. I haven't seen you in what, like a day or two," he said, pulling me tighter. Really, it had been at least a week. My father was a head surgeon at the Cranbrook Hospital, so he was extremely busy. When he did come home, I didn't see him because I was usually sleeping when he came in and still asleep when he left for work. But what could you do, he was still my father.

My mother leaned leisurely next to my father with a disapproving look. I didn't know whether the look was because I tackled my father in a hug, which was very unladylike, or because I didn't give her a hug. Maybe if she didn't act like such a bitch, I would. I released my father, shying away, going back to stand next to my grandmother. My mother's eyes followed me. "I guess Gwen didn't do such a bad job."

"Yeah, sweetheart. You look lovely." My father commented, not even looking at me but at his iPhone. He was here, but he really wasn't. My grandma scoffed beside me. I smirked; at least I wasn't the only one who thought my parents were incompetent.

My mother suddenly squealed, waving her hands. "I forgot to tell you," she started, really directing her statement toward my father and Grandma. "The mixer this month is, too, held by, wait for it...me!"

The mixer was a party that was held by one of the members of the country club. It was a big deal, I guess, within the country club. The host would plan a big soiree with little finger sandwiches and fruity drinks—the whole nine yards. And this year, it would be held in our backyard.

I tried not to groan out loud. "Fran said she wanted to help out some, so I invited her to dinner today."

Oh, this is too good. Now, I must put on a show for some unknown people. I'll do what always seems to work for me. Stay invisible.

~

Mother liked my outfit so much, she made me change, which made no sense whatsoever. If she thought I looked so "daring," why couldn't I just wear what I had on? But now, she wanted to show off for Grandma and whoever that Fran lady was.

Gwen arrived home from school and soon came to dress me instructed by my mother. She was more than happy to play dress up. She came into my room with a simple black peplum dress laid over her arm, a pair of black suede pumps hanging from her fingers, and her pink curling iron.

I put on the dress without any refusal, knowing it would be completely useless. Then I sat in a chair for at least an hour as Gwen curled my hair. When she finished, she pinned the right side of my hair back. I slipped on the heels and walked over to my full-length mirror. When I saw myself, I grimaced.

"You don't look bad. Actually, you looked better than I do," she said with a hint of jealousy. "You're not even trying, and you looked gorgeous." Gwen came and stood behind me. She was usually taller than me, but the heels made us have the same height

"What could make this better?" she said with sympathy. A new family, maybe? But I wouldn't say that out loud because I knew it might hurt Gwen's feelings. They have no support whatsoever. Gwen sighed, pushing her hair behind her ear. "Well, how about your glasses back? I found where Mom was hiding them. Her purse wasn't such a smart place."

I smiled at my sister widely in the mirror. "Thank you."

"No problem. I know how much you hate dressing like this. I just thought your glasses would make you feel a bit normal." She took my glasses out of her purse and handed them to me. I quickly took the contacts out of my eyes and slipped on my glasses. I sighed out loud, glad to be with them again.

"Now I must change. I'm going to try to look sexier than you do. Let's hope I can pull it off." I still stood in the mirror when Gwen left the room. I guess she was right, though. I did look nice, in a way.

I picked up my phone and snapped a picture of myself. As I sent it to Neal, I could hear the front door slam and mumbles of chatter coming from the foyer. The guests are here.

I had no interest in going to meet the guests, so I camped out on the edge of my bed. A few minutes later, Neal texted back.

Neal: *Whoa, sexy mama! ;)*

Me: *I wanted to show you what my mother did this time.*

Neal: *What's the special occasion?*

Me: *Country club people are coming over. Some lady named Fran, and most likely her husband. You know how they come in pairs.*

"Josephine! The guests are here," I heard my mother shout in a sweet voice. But I could tell she was agitated. With a huff, I slipped my phone in my pocket before going into the hall.

I could feel my phone vibrate. My heels clicked on the wooden floor as I walked, announcing my entrance. I decided that I would be rude and answer my phone while at the top of the stairs.

Neal: *You mean, Francine Winchester????*

My eyes widened. Holy fuck. Excuse my language.

CHAPTER 9
Are You Stalking Me?

I whipped my head up from the text on my phone. There in my foyer stood a well-dressed woman and a tailored man chatting with my parents. Beside them, staring at me, was Olivia.

She always seemed to pop up at the most inconvenient times. It was as if she did it on purpose.

I took a shaky breath nervously and descended the half spiral stairs. Oh my God, Olivia was in my house. Here I was, hyperventilating, but she had already been in my house once before. Though she had only been here for a couple of minutes, it still counted. Now, she would be here having dinner with my family and me.

As I walked slowly, my mother spared a glance my way. "Here's my other daughter now." She scowled when she saw my glasses perched on my nose. "My mother had prepared food in the kitchen. Why don't we take this into the dining area?"

The Winchesters followed my parents willingly into the dining room except for Olivia.

She stood at the base of the stairs with a hand on the banister; her brown eyes were sparkling as she looked at me. She smiled—the smile she seemed to had reserved for me and only me.

Olivia wore a light purple shirtwaist dress with a white belt around her midsection. Her white multi-strap heels made her legs look as if they ran for days. Olivia's brown locks were curled, resting lazily down her back.

She was gorgeous.

I could not help but smile a little. When I reached the end, I stood on the last stair, eye level with Olivia's. I liked being her height.

"Hi," Olivia said with her glowing smile. "You look beautiful." Her eyes flickered down my body.

I blushed heavily and bashfully looked down at my heels. "T-thanks." I wanted to tell her how stunning I thought she looked, but I couldn't get the words out.

Olivia reached out and tucked a blonde strand behind my ear like she did the day I fell unconscious.

Olivia must have liked seeing me blush because her action only caused me to blush harder. Her heavenly laugh filled the foyer. "I swear, you're so cute."

I smiled at her, trying to cover up my nervousness. The butterflies in my stomach were flying over the place.

Olivia held out her left hand towards me, palm up. "M'lady."

I stared at her hand, hesitant to take it. Olivia nodded in reassurance, still with a large smile. "This last step could be dangerous for a woman like yourself," she said with a funny medieval British accent. I giggled a little in my hand.

She was right. I would be the one to trip and break something on one stair.

I slowly placed my hand in hers. She gently tugged on my hand, helping me lower myself to the wooden floor in heels.

"Shall we?"

I nodded, still not being able to form words with her in such proximity. She tugged on my hand, dragging me toward the dining area. Olivia's hand felt warm and soft in mine. When we reached the door, she dropped my hand. I frowned at the loss of contact.

There were only two chairs left when we arrived, obviously, for Olivia and me. The room was decorated with cream-colored carpet, a long mahogany table paired with eight white suede chairs, and a medium-sized crystal chandelier hung elegantly at the center.

Not wanting to be noticed, I went over to my chair with my head hanging. Olivia was right behind me, striding confidently to the seat next to mine. I sat in my chair, and Olivia sat in hers.

Our parents paid no attention to us, chatting away, laughing and just having a jolly old good time. It looked as if no work was being done for the mixer. It just seemed like they were gossiping like usual. My grandma sat quietly, eating the roasted chicken, string beans, and mashed potatoes that she had cooked. My grandma didn't really favor high society life like my mother did.

When Olivia and I had sat, my grandma gave me a pointed look—which I really didn't understand—with an eyebrow raised. I looked at her, confused, not understanding what she was trying to say. She smiled slightly, shook her head, and went back to her food.

"This meal is lovely," Olivia piped up, speaking to my grandma.

Grandmother just said with an uninterested glance, not one for small talk, "Thank you, dear." I stayed quiet, not really having anything to say.

"Are you and Joey friends?" my grandmother inquired.

Olivia chewed her food slowly, contemplating what to say next. "In a way." She shot a quick smile at me as if saying 'I know something you don't.' Whatever it was, I wanted to know about it.

"What does 'in a way' mean?" my grandma asked, squinting her eyes at Olivia, analyzing her. What was my grandma doing?

"Yes, she is my friend, unless she doesn't think so." My grandma sat there for a moment, staring at Olivia. Olivia just smiled under her gaze.

"Okay. It's good that Joey is making friends. She usually is only with that Neal boy."

My mother extracted herself quickly from the conversation when she heard the word Neal and friends in the same sentence. "Neal and Josephine aren't going to be friends anymore, isn't that right?"

Gwen started coughing across from me, which was a much-needed distraction. I tried to avoid the question by eating food on my plate, but literally, everyone at the table was looking at me, even Olivia.

"Um, no. I-I don't like N-Neal l like that," I said. My mother scoffed with a frown. Next to her, my father was typing something on his phone. Gwen looked...relieved? The Winchesters just really didn't care. Grandma looked slightly confused. Moreover, Olivia looked like she was struggling to hold back a grin.

Why must my mother only speak to me when it involves my personal life?

Quietness, as well as awkwardness, settled over the table as we all finished our dinner.

"Well, that was just delicious," my father spoke, saying his first words, acknowledging the entire table.

"How about we finish the night with a dessert?" my mother said.

I took that as my cue to leave. I didn't want to sit through another meal with the likes of my parents. "M-may I be excused?"

My mother glared at me. I knew she was criticizing my nervous habit. Father was back to typing on his phone already.

"If you must," she answered curtly.

"H-have a nice evening everyone," I said before quickly pushing my chair back. I only made to the exit when Olivia spoke.

"May I come with you?" Olivia asked politely. My face screwed up with confusion as I gawked at Olivia. Did she just ask if she could come with me to my room? Maybe she didn't know I was retreating to my room. Nope, I was pretty sure she did.

"W-why—" I started, but my mother cut me off quickly. *Bitch.*

"She would love to have you."

Nevertheless, Olivia clearly didn't care for my mother's response. She cocked her head to the side, waiting for mine. I didn't really have time to think over rather or not should I let Olivia come into my room, so I just nodded. A smile bloomed on her face as she followed me out the room.

The trek to my room was a quiet one. All we could hear was each other's footsteps. I nervously placed my hand on the doorknob. This was the first time I have had anyone besides Neal and my family inside my room.

What the heck, what is the worst that could happen? I opened the door, gesturing for Olivia to go first. I could hear her gasp as she entered. Oh, great. I left it a mess, and now Olivia thought I was a gross slob.

I followed behind her. My room wasn't that messy. Well at least, that's what I had thought. I rushed around, cleaning up the clothes that were littered all over the floor and threw them in my hamper.

Olivia stood in the middle of the spacious room, staring at all the items in the room. "This is amazing," she said in awe. I think she was referring to all the photos I had on my wall.

I cleared my throat before speaking. "Umm, thanks."

"I didn't know you liked photography this much. It's incredible," she said, going over to the wall to examine the photos. She walked slowly around the room, looking at every bulletin board and picture frame. I stood nervously, wringing my hands. No one has ever really looked at my photos, once again, besides Neal. She paused when she got to one photo, which I could not see over her shoulder.

"Are you stalking me?"

"What?" I squeaked out, not understanding.

"Are you stalking me?" Olivia said much slower this time as if slowing down her words would help me understand.

"N-no, I'm not stalking you." The funny thing about this conversation was that if anything, it was her stalking me—always popping up at my house, leaving candy in my locker, holding my nose to stop it from bleeding, standing in a long line just to give me a sweet kiss…Wait what was I talking about?

Yes, she was the one stalking me, not the other way around.

"Well, this photo I have here says otherwise," Olivia said with a hint of amusement.

"What photo?"

"This photo," she answered, walking away from the wall toward me, holding the picture out. I took it from her cautiously. The first thing I thought when I looked at it was maybe I was stalking her and I didn't know it.

It was a picture of Olivia sitting at a stone table, though I assumed it to be in the courtyard at school. But this wasn't the same Olivia that stood in front of me now. This one seemed a little younger. I could tell because her hair was shorter and she had somewhat of a baby face. She had her hand under her chin with a distant look in her eyes.

I remembered when I took this picture. It was freshman year, and I first discovered what a great view the hill had. I was there one day, overlooking the courtyard when I saw Olivia. She looked so disconnected and somewhat lonely. It was at least the second week of school, so she did not have her usual pack of girls around. It was probably the only time I had ever seen her alone. I had forgotten I had it. I didn't even know how to explain why I had taken it.

"I-I don't know why I have it."

"Someone seemed to be infatuated with me," Olivia said with a singsong voice, laughing. I even smiled a little.

"I'm not. I take a lot of photos. You just happen to be one of my subjects at the time," I said, taking the picture back to its place on its bulletin board.

Olivia chuckled, running her hand through her hair. "I think I liked it better when you were infatuated with me, rather than me just being some random subject," she said, sounding a little defeated.

I wanted to reassure and tell her that she was not just a subject in a picture. But I couldn't. I wasn't ready to. I decided to be bold and tell her something else. "You're my friend. In a way." I cracked a smile, repeating her words.

"Do you even know what I meant by 'in a way?'" Olivia said, taking steps toward me with a flirty tone. I gulped, suddenly becoming nervous. She was so close again. The scent of mint and lilac clouded my nose. Why did she always smell like that?

"N-no."

"Do you want me to tell you what it means?" she whispered. However, she was close enough for me to hear her loud and clear. Olivia's big soft brown eyes were set on me, flickering from my eyes to my lips. She didn't wait for my answer. "It means—"

"Olivia!" A voice called from downstairs, breaking the trance. Olivia groaned and closed her eyes. "Really," she mumbled, exasperated.

"Olivia!" the voice called again.

"I'm coming!" A heavy sigh escaped Olivia's mouth; she clearly looked annoyed.

Olivia's eyes softened again as she looked at me. Gently, she put a hand on my left cheek and leaned in. My heart was beating so fast, I swear it was going to pop out any minute now. Ever so slowly, she placed a soft lingering kiss on my cheek.

"Maybe next time," she whispered in my ear. When she pulled away, I could still feel her breath on my ear. Olivia looked at me one last time before sauntering out of the room.

I stood there, stunned. I took a nervous breath, not knowing what to do with myself. I felt all scrambled, and everything felt intense. My whole body felt hot and tingly. The only thing I kept thinking was *what a tease.*

Wait, did I want her to kiss me? Would it have been so wrong if I did?

CHAPTER 10
Mixing It Up

After Olivia left, I took a cold shower to get my body back to its normal temperature and not the warm feeling I felt all over. Although, I kind of liked it.

My parents went back to their usual routines: on their phones, thinking about themselves, and ignoring me.

And as usual, I couldn't care less. It's sad, really, because they're my family; I should care about whether or not they wanted to spend time with me, but after seventeen years, I got over it.

My sister told me she was going out (same old, same old). When I asked her where she was going, she gave me some cryptic ass answer. I thought about her answer for the first five seconds then shrugged it off five seconds later. Like I mentioned before, I no longer care.

The cold shower left its expected effect. I was freezing, so my remedy was to curl on the couch with a warm blanket and pop in *Beauty and the Beast*. I did have my Snuggie at first, but then I tripped because that thing was way longer than I was. I tossed it back in my closet.

I snuggled deeper in the couch, eyes focused on Beast and Belle dancing in the ballroom. On the outside, their world seems as perfect as Disney movies portrayed. But I knew on the inside, they were miserable, and only their love for each other was the cure.

In a way, as I stared at Beast as he looks at Belle, I realized Beast and I were alike in some aspects. Both of us were

69

rejected by society because of our appearances and hard yet shy exteriors. The difference between us though was he had found love, and I have not. Oh, and that he is a giant hairy monster with conceited ways and a temper.

Maybe all I needed to do was find my Belle, and life would get better. My mind drifted from the fairytale couple to Olivia.

She was always so forward and confident, not afraid to show everyone who she was. Olivia could like whoever she wanted when she wanted. She was so beautiful and yet so humble. Olivia was the best of both worlds. But she still bothered to be near me. It was a mystery.

Olivia could turn me into a nervous stuttering mess with just one look. And for some reason, it wasn't like the scared nervousness I get around others; it was more like an excited jittery feeling. I sort of even liked it.

"What were you thinking about so hard, kangaroo? I'm sure a Disney movie is not that philosophical."

I turned my head away from the screen. I could see a smile on my grandma's face due to the illuminating TV screen, but her eyes shone with slight concern.

"Nothing important."

"Fine. Do you mind if watch with you? There is nothing to do around here," my grandma said before plopping down next to me on the couch, not waiting for an invitation.

We sat in silence staring at the TV.

"So, what's up with that Olivia girl? She seemed like a little snob," Grandma said, breaking the silence.

"She's not like that!" I defended quickly with vigor. My grandma stared at me in shock because I rarely ever raise my voice. I blushed heavily under my grandma's gaze. "I-I mean she is not a snob. Olivia is really nice, I g-guess."

"So, she is your friend then?" I nodded and returned my gaze to the TV, trying to avoid the conversation altogether.

70

"I don't think she is your friend," Grandma spoke, bringing up Olivia again. I sighed; she apparently wasn't going to let my outburst go.

"But she is."

"I think there is something going on between you two, but I won't say anything because you haven't figured it out for yourself yet."

My eyes widened, catching on to what she was implying. Did she think I liked Olivia in that way?

"I d-don't—"

She cut me off, raising her hand. I shut my mouth quickly.

"I do want you to know that I will support your decisions no matter what happens. Okay?" Grandma said with kind eyes. I knew she would be there for me always, but in this instance, I didn't know exactly what she meant.

"Okay," I answered anyways, not even putting up a fight.

"Well, now that it is settled, I don't think I can stomach any more of this Disney garbage any longer."

"It's not garbage. It's magic," I said stubbornly. How dare she insult my Disney?

"Whatever you say, kangaroo. I'm going to sleep. This old bat can't stay on her feet any longer." Grandma leaned over and kissed me on the forehead before getting up and heading to the guest room.

I slouched back into the couch, no longer tensed from the conversation I just had. I was about to start watching the film again, but then I began thinking.

Did she only come into the living room to talk to me about Olivia?

~

When Saturday—the day of the mixer—had arrived, in my large spacious backyard milled all types of employees.

71

Bartenders, waiters, caters, musicians—you name it, they were there.

I could see tables with white tablecloth and decorative flowers set on each one from my window. Slow classical music along with my mother's voice floated up to my window. My mother was running around, frantically shouting orders at people left and right.

I had already been dressed in a white strapless floral-print dress. It was paired with a pale pink cardigan so I wasn't too exposed. It matched the array of light blue, green, yellow, and pink flowers on the dress.

My hair was pulled up into a messy bun with strands of hair loosened around my face and the base of my neck.

As usual, I was uncomfortable as hell. This mixer would be just like the carnival, maybe even worst. There would be tons and tons of high society families and their children everywhere. I would be on full display because my mother was the hostess. She would take every chance she could get to brag about how glamorous her life was.

At least Neal would be there. There was some comfort in that. He would be there for me if things got too overwhelming.

Oh, and let's not forget Olivia would, of course, be there, adding on comfort and pressure at the same time.

Looking out the window once more, I could see clusters of people arriving. I knew I better get downstairs, knowing my mother wanted me to stand there and be bragged about.

I slipped on some white sandals that had been set out for me before making my way downstairs. I slowly walked down the stairs, continuing my way to the foyer when I heard someone calling my name.

"Joey!" Neal yelled through the halls. I followed his voice and found him standing in the kitchen, stuffing his face with little finger sandwiches that were on the many plates on the counters. When he saw me, he cackled with laughter.

"Again? When do you think your mother will get tired of playing 'Dress up with Joey?'"

"Soon, I hope," I said, stealing a finger sandwich from his hand and taking a bite. "Where's your mom?"

Neal cringed at the fact that I was talking with my mouth full. "She's around. Close your mouth!"

I shrugged, eating more food from the other plates.

"So…" Neal dragged out, mischief dancing in his eyes.

"So, what?"

"So, Olivia was here, having dinner with you and your family. Was she able to keep her hands off your sexy body?"

A familiar, rosy scarlet color spread over my cheeks, remembering the fact that she really didn't keep to herself.

"Nothing happened," I mumbled, no longer interested in eating since my stomach was now full of butterflies.

"Just you saying nothing happened clues me in on the fact that something happened."

"Can we talk about this later? Possibly, when the whole damn country is not in our backyard."

"We will talk about this Olivia thing later," Neal said with a serious voice, all jokes aside.

"Yes, we will." And we would. I needed to talk to someone about her. The situation was all so confusing; my emotions were all over the place. I need to get them out and get honest insight in return. I knew Neal would give me just that.

"Good. Now let's go find a better food to eat and bother rich stuck-up aristocrats."

~

It had been at least two hours already, and I was ready to stab someone with one of the sterling silver forks. I can't tell you how many times I had to shake someone's hand with an overly fake smile.

I was dragged a couple of times by my mother to meet whoever she wanted to impress at the time. I was told at least

73

fifty times to stand up straight, and ten times, some polo-wearing douchebag tried to look up my dress.

Neal ditched me halfway through the meet and greet, running off saying something about wanting to see somebody. Some help he was.

I was ready to crawl into a hole and die. To make it all worst, I hadn't even seen Olivia yet.

Now, I sat alone at one of the tables, staring up at the sky. I was glad I was finally able to get a break.

Out of the corner of my eye, I could see Neal leaning on the white fence that surrounded the backyard talking to some girl, who was leaning awfully close to him. I curiously raised an eyebrow trying to see who the girl was. I almost fell out of my chair when I noticed the girl had an identical blonde hair to mine. Gwendolyn reached out and grabbed Neal's hand, holding it in both of hers. He smiled cheerfully, eating it up.

What the heck! When did this happen? I can't even right now. I could feel a small headache creeping up into my head. I would definitely talk to him about it when we have our serious talk later.

"Already tired of the high society scene, are we?" a melodic voice spoke from behind me. I quickly whipped around to look in the face of Olivia. She stood there, a vision in a light blue vintage dress with large pink roses everywhere.

A large smile stretched across her tan face. The light was shining on her face, so she was forced to squint her eyes, but I was still able to see her honey brown orbs. With the light shining on them, I could also see green bursting from her black pupils. I could sit there and stare at her for days.

I smiled an identical smile, I would even admit to the fact that I was so happy to see her.

"Where have you been? I was looking for you everywhere," Olivia said, taking a seat next to me, propping her elbow up on the table and putting her head in her hand. Her shiny brown hair flew gracefully onto her smooth arm.

74

"I've been around, shaking hands here and there."

"Sounds like tons of fun," she said, mocking me.

"It really was, but I had to take a break from all the excitement," I said, sighing loudly while rubbing my temples.

"If you really do need to rest, I can leave," Olivia said, rising from her seat a little. I rose, placing my hand on her arm. Her eyes left my eyes to look at my hand resting on her arm. A small smile slowly came onto her face.

"No!" I said in a high-pitched voice. Olivia looked at me with an amused grin. "N-no, you can stay. I'm fine."

"You know, I have noticed you always say that you're fine when you're not. How come you never let someone worry about you?"

My face hardened as we both sat back in our chairs. I looked around our backyard, trying to avoid answering, staring at everyone milling around, chatting, eating, and drinking.

"People don't worry about me," I said, not really wanting to continue talking about this topic. Olivia seemed to get it well enough even though she still looked curious.

"Did I forget to tell you that you look lovely?" As usual, Olivia could make me go from slightly confident to a nervous mess. I ducked my head to hide my blush from her. She let out a soft laugh, bending her head, trying to catch my eye.

"T-thanks," I said, looking at her through my eyelashes shyly. Olivia stared back boldly, shifting closer to me.

"Am I interrupting something?" a confident voice spoke. Olivia and I slowly dragged our eyes away from each other to look at the intruder. I was surprised to see Danika standing there with her hands on her hips in a black lace dress and red pumps. She was probably the only person in our backyard wearing such dark colors.

"Yes, you are," Olivia bit out, clearly annoyed. She stood to her full height, squaring off with Danika. Olivia's nostrils flared, and her eyes flashed with anger as she looked at

Danika. Danika just stood there, smiling innocently like she didn't know what she was doing. What was she doing?

"Well golly, I'm sorry. I didn't mean to. I just wanted to see what you two kids are up to," Danika said, flashing her pearly whites again.

"Nothing of your concern," Olivia said rudely, still staring Danika down. I just sat there beneath them as they had their showdown for whatever reason.

Danika, chillingly rubbing her arms, said, "Burr, chilly today, aren't we? Really, I came over here to invite you to the after party," she said, fixing her gaze on me, making the question directed at me. But I sat there, confused.

"There is an after party?" I spoke up finally.

"Yeah, at Nolan Grace's house. You in?"

Nolan Grace was one of the big shot all-star super hottie lacrosse players at Cranbrook High school. He threw huge parties at his mansion every so often. Nolan was almost as popular as Olivia. Almost.

"Well…" I started off. I didn't really like parties. Well, come to think of it, I have never been invited or have gone to a party. How would I know if I liked them or not?

"Would you like to go?" Olivia asked me.

I paused for a moment. I guess I could try it. I nodded, confirming my answer. Danika squealed a little, clapping her hands.

"Great! I'll see you there," she said, directing her excitement toward me. I noticed that Danika really doesn't talk to Olivia when she was around. She left soon after, swinging her hips as she walked away.

Olivia wiped her face with her hands, mumbling what sounded like the word *bitch*. But I wasn't sure.

She sat down again next to me, her brown eyes seeming calm now that Danika had left. "Looks like we're going to a party."

A party could be fun, I guess.

76

CHAPTER 11
Who Wants to Party?

The party didn't start until the mixer was near its end, so naturally, my mother found me again smiling widely at Olivia and whisked me off to chat with more country club members. I was sure Gwen would have been more than enough to brag about. My mother must have been tired of pretending she only had one child.

But not before Olivia smiled like she had a secret and whispered in my ear, "I'll find you later." I believed her. If she didn't find me later, I would be surprised since she always had a knack for knowing where I was.

Neal kept hanging around Gwen when he could and laughing at my misfortune until his mother slapped him on the head, scolding him for joking around too much. I was grateful.

When I noticed that the partygoers were soon leaving and the sun was setting, I detached myself from my mother's clutches to find Neal.

Neal was sitting at a table with his eyes closed, steadily breathing, feeling the effects of the mixer. I made my way over to him. I stopped my movements when I noticed Gwen making her way over, holding drinks in her hand.

I really didn't know what to do when I saw them. It felt awkward. Neal never dated or showed interest in other girls except when we were, like, ten. He admitted to liking me, but I punched him in the stomach. Then we went back to being best friends.

Now, he was being all chummy with my sister. Since when did she like younger skinny red heads that couldn't play a sport to save his life? Neal was far from Gwen's usually masculine meathead type. Gwen liked guys that had brawns instead of brain.

Really, the only problem I had with the situation was that fact that Neal never even told me something was going on between the two of them. I felt a little betrayed and altogether confused.

I was jolted out of my thoughts when a warm hand slid onto my back, pulling me to them. I knew who it was before I even looked at her face. Olivia never paid any attention to someone else's boundaries.

"Why the long face? I know this mixer isn't your scene, but it's not that bad." Well, she was right about the mixer; it wasn't my scene. But considering her mother wasn't like mine, she wasn't forced to show off constantly. She could have fun with all these people she knew. To Olivia, it wasn't that bad; but to a social outcast like me, it was.

"I'm not sad about the mixer," I said, eyes flickering to Neal. Olivia followed my gaze over to the couple. A frown appeared on her face just like mine.

"Wait, I thought you said you didn't like Neal," Olivia said with sadness coating her voice as she retracted her arm from around my waist. I grabbed her hand unconsciously, pulling her back to me.

"I don't!" I said quickly, trying to clarify. "It's just that I didn't know about them being together. Neal didn't tell me."

"Oh, I get it," Olivia said calmer, now willingly leaning back into me. Her body, distracting me for a moment, felt warm next to mine. "If one of my friends didn't tell me they had a thing for someone, I would be hurt too. On top of that, the girl he has a thing for is your sister. It's like how Danika…" Her face screwed up weirdly before she said, "You know what, it

78

doesn't even matter. How about we invite them to the after party?"

"Gwen has probably already been invited, knowing her."

"Well, what about Neal? He probably doesn't want to go, but if he knows you are, then he will." She made a good point, and I would like to have at least someone besides Olivia at the party. Also, it seemed pretty logical because Olivia smiled at me with her big brown eyes sparkling. I couldn't help but (in so many words) melt.

My body felt even warmer than it had before. I knew she was standing close to me, but she was standing super close to me in a crowd full of sticking-their-nose-in-other-people's-business type of people. I felt self-conscious, knowing people could see us. But I got over it to marvel at the fact of how soft Olivia's hair looked.

I shook my head, realizing that I was staring at her hair unabashedly. Now bashfully, I ducked my head away from her and nodded shyly. Olivia happily clamped onto my arm and dragged me toward Neal and Gwen.

When we arrived at the table, Neal stood up, acknowledging my presence. "Hey, Joey. Enjoying the gala?" he said, using his best British accent. I think the British accent was like a running gag of his.

Even though I was still a little upset about the whole Gwen thing, I knew he would talk to me about it later, so it was fine. With a British accent matching his, I said, "Just fabulous. The food was simply delightful. Don't you agree?"

"I do concur. I did enjoy the—" He was about to say something else when Gwen cut him off.

"Guys, seriously?" she said, getting up to stand next to him.

Neal's lightly freckled face began to turn a pinkish color. I put my hand over my mouth to keep from laughing at his embarrassment. Usually, I was the one that was embarrassed; now it was his turn.

Neal stuffed his hands in his nicely-pressed khakis, pretending to act cool, trying to preserve his dignity that was almost shattered by his silliness. "What's up?"

I shrugged with a smile, still amused. "Nothing."

Olivia nudged me in the side. "Actually, we wanted to see if you guys were going to the after party."

Gwen tried not to look smug, but she came off as smug anyways. "Nolan already asked me." I shot a pointed look at Olivia. "But Neal refuses to go with me."

Neal took his hands out of his pockets, crossing his arms across his scrawny chest, clearly angry. "That jackass didn't invite me. He only invited you." I raised an eyebrow at his tone. Someone was jealous. I had to stifle another laugh. I thought, *I'm going to like this whole Neal crushing on my sister thing—after I get over the fact that his crush is my sister.*

"That jackass didn't say I couldn't bring a guest," Gwen rebutted, lightly placing her manicured hand on his arm.

"If it counts for anything, Joey and I are going," Olivia added.

"What?" Gwen said, taking herself away from Neal. "What do you mean you're going?"

"W-Well, um, Danika invited me." Olivia scowled at Danika's name.

Gwen let out an exasperated sigh. "What does that little harlot get off inviting you? And why did you agree? You don't like parties. Something could happen to you especially since you've never even been to a party before." Worry was coming off her in heavy waves. At least I could tell she cared.

"I, uh, was going w-with Olivia." Olivia blushed a little, but she still stared at Gwen head on. Gwen stared back, scrutinizing Olivia where she stood. The air was thick with awkwardness until Neal nudged Gwen in the back, raising his eyebrows with meaning. I really didn't understand what he was trying to tell her, but she understood because her mouth dropped in an 'O' shape and she nodded.

She turned her attention back to Olivia, still holding a glare. Olivia decided that would be the best time to let Gwen win their little stare off by breaking eye contact with her. Gwen pointed a finger at Olivia accusingly. "You better look out for her."

Olivia nodded quickly. "I will."

Neal sighed heavily, wiping his face with his hand. "I'll go too, I guess." Gwen squealed at this, finally taking her attention off Olivia. I could hear a small sigh escape from Olivia's mouth, but she smiled at me in reassurance to let me know she was okay with Gwen's interrogation.

"Yay! We're going to a party!" Gwen squealed again with excitement. "This is going to be so much fun."

I sure hoped it would be.

CHAPTER 12
Fruit Punch

As soon as the mixer was over, Neal and I were clear to go. We all piled into Olivia's 2016 Chevy Equinox with me in the front with Olivia, then Neal and Gwen in the back.

The ride to Nolan's was quiet except for Neal and Gwen's constant banter in the back.

I felt nervous about this party because of course, this was my first one, and I had no idea what it would be like. I sat, wringing my hands on my lap, trying to get rid of my nervous tension.

At a red light, out of my peripheral vision, I could see Olivia taking her eyes off the road to spare a glance at me. But I didn't return her gaze because I was too focused on the nerves building steadily in my stomach.

A smile appeared on Olivia's face as she reached out and grabbed my hand. I pulled my eyes up to look at her. She just gave me a wide smile, eyes sparkling. Olivia looked so stunning with the street lights shining softly on the side of her face, making her eyes look even prettier than they already were. Her hand fit perfectly within mine; it was the perfect distraction.

"It will be fine."

When the light turned green, Olivia dragged our joined hands to the middle of the car console to rest comfortably between us. Olivia had solved the problem of distracting me of my nerves, but now I was hyper-aware of how her hand felt.

I could hear Neal snickering in the backseat, along with Gwen. But I ignored them and focused on Olivia beside me.

A while later, we pulled up to Nolan's house. Cars were lined up and down the street, stretching even farther away from Nolan's mansion. Music boomed from the house to the point where it could be heard throughout the neighborhood. No one seemed to be saying anything about noise control though. Teenagers were everywhere in and outside the house.

My nerves built up again regardless of the fact that Olivia was holding my hand. We clambered out the car slowly, in awe of our crazy surroundings.

"Whoa, what a party," Neal said, staring at the teens running past with shoes on their hands and towels tied around their necks, shouting random things. It was some party.

"A-are they always like this?" I stammered, asking no one in general.

Gwen pumped her fist in the air with a wild grin. "Hell yes! I need alcohol," she said, grabbing Neal's wrist, pulling him to the front door. Before they entered, Gwen turned back, giving Olivia a pointed glare. Olivia nodded in return.

When they were out of sight, Olivia held out her hand in front of me, urging me to take it. I hesitated at first because we would be holding hands in front of the entire student body, but then I realized everyone was either passed out or wasted, so it wouldn't matter. I took it.

Olivia danced excitedly on the balls of her toes, then she tugged me toward the house. On the way to the door, we both got sidetracked, looking at the guys standing on the second-floor balcony railing. There was a crowd of people below him, loudly chanting, "Do it!" He did it alright. He catapulted himself off the balcony and into the crowd below. Luckily, they caught him.

A *wow* escaped my mouth as I stared at the crowd, clapping the guy on his back.

"Wow indeed. Let's go." Olivia agreed before continuing our trek inside the house. I gasped when we entered.

Outside the house was nothing compared to its inside. Olivia smirked as she let me take in the sight.

I didn't know what to expect, but I sure wasn't prepared for what I saw. People were literally everywhere. People occupied every single room in the house. The rooms that used to be the living and dining room now doubled as a super crowded, sweaty dance floor. The kitchen was packed with people, food, and alcohol. Horny teenagers were occupying every spot possible. A trail of people stood, chatting and drinking on the stairs.

By looking at the scene before me, I concluded I dislike parties. I was so out of my comfort zone here. I liked to be by myself with a calming environment, not a massive house with raging crazy loud teens.

People got even rowdier when they heard a remixed dance version of Mr. Saxobeat by Alexandra Stan. The music bounced off the walls loudly along with multicolored strobe lights.

"This is crazy," I said, still in awe of my surroundings.

"What?" Olivia shouted, trying to be heard over the loud music.

"Forget it!" I shouted back. Talking in this noise was obviously useless, but it seemed like no one wanted to. I was sure if you asked the couple who were making out intensely to my right, they would agree.

"Want to get something to drink?" Olivia shouted, cupping her hands over her mouth so that I could hear her better. I nodded, knowing my small voice would not be heard.

Olivia clutched my hand tighter as we started through the monstrous crowd of people. I was afraid I might get lost in this huge mess. I bumped into so many people before we finally made it over to the kitchen. I didn't even bother to apologize.

In the kitchen, we went over to the counter with red solo cups piled high. Olivia grabbed two, then we went over to where the drinks were set out. There were two punch bowls that were surrounded by various bottles of alcohol. One bowl was labeled *Safe*, and the other was labeled *Not so safe*. I pointed to the *Safe* one. Since I have never had alcohol, I didn't think now would not be a good time to try it.

Olivia got our drinks while I took the time to scope out the kitchen. The kitchen seemed to be in the same position as the rest of the house, minus the crazed dancing. As I was looking around, I could see somebody waving, apparently, at me.

Through the dimmed lights, I could see that it was Danika. She was leaning against some guy while giving me a sultry smile. The guy also followed her line of vision and looked at me. It felt more like leering by the way his eyes were moving down my body. He finally took his gaze off me to whisper something in Danika's ear. She nodded, but she still stared at me with dark eyes.

Shyly, I turned back to Olivia and focused on her, not Danika and her guy friend.

Olivia handed me my drink not a second later. I didn't take a sip because I was too focused on not spilling it since people were bumping me left and right.

"Want to dance?" Olivia shouted before sipping her red solo cup.

"Um well, I'm like incapable of dancing." Which was true, since I was naturally a klutz. I always tripped over my own two feet along with everyone else's.

"I'm sure you're not that bad," Olivia said, trying to reassure me. She wouldn't if she had ever seen me dance.

"No really, I can't dance."

"Okay, it's fine. I won't pressure you. We can have fun doing other things," Olivia said slowly, looking at me through her eyelashes. My face was coated with blush, catching what she had really meant by 'other things.'

Before I could even say anything back, we were interrupted by the high-pitched squeals of two girls. I flinched

85

when the screams got even closer. The squealers turned out to be Cassidy and Jocelyn. They ran over to Olivia, tackling her in a hug and completely ignoring me just like the last time we had an encounter.

"Oh my God! You came!" Cassidy yelled with excitement. From the way her eyes were glazed over and the dopey smile she had plastered on her face, I could tell she was drunk. Same goes for Jocelyn. They still weren't drunk enough to actually talk to me.

"We didn't think you were coming!" Jocelyn yelled in an equally loud voice.

"Well, here I am, with Joey," Olivia said with a slight cringe, clearly affected by their loud voices. Cassidy and Jocelyn both stopped hugging Olivia and looked at me. Their excitement vanished and was replaced with indifference. As quickly as I had gotten their attention, they focused back on Olivia.

"Let's go dance," Cassidy suggested while teetering off to the side a little bit.

"I can't. Like I said, I'm here with Joey."

"Ugh!" Jocelyn groaned annoyed. "You're so killing my buzz. Come on, come dance with us." Olivia looked at me to see what I would say. I didn't mind if she went to go dance. I didn't want to ruin her fun just because I was accident prone. The only thing about it was that I would be left alone. But Olivia really looked like she wanted to go and dance.

"Okay."

"Are you sure? I could—"

Cassidy cut her off, not being able to wait any longer. "She said it's fine. Let's go!"

"But—" Olivia started to protest, but I cut her off this time.

"It's okay. I'll just be outside. I think I need some air anyway."

86

Olivia didn't look so convinced but nodded anyway. Then she let herself be dragged off in the raging crowd of dancing people. I sighed, now I was alone. I honestly had no idea where Neal was by now. There were too many people to be sure. Not that I was worried or anything. I was sure Gwen was with him so he would be fine, so I wasn't going to waste time looking for him. I really did want to get some air since it was getting hot in there.

I set my drink down, not really wanting it any longer since it was tepid and watered down by the ice cubes.

I shuffled my way through the thick, congested crowd over to a sliding door that led outside. I slid it open and walked into the crisp night. Some people were already outside hanging out, but it wasn't that many, so I wasn't bothered.

I went over to the railing on the wooden porch to lean against it. The view was of a big dark forest. It wasn't scary looking though; it was more serene. I breathed in deeply, taking in the chilly air and the smell of the forest.

I was brought back to the party when someone cleared their throat behind me, succeeding in scaring the shit out of me as well. I turned to see the guy that was standing with Danika earlier, holding two red solo cups.

"Can I join you?" he asked, coming to stand next to me, even though I didn't tell him he could.

"Here, have a drink," the guy said, giving me one of the red solo cups. "I'm Nolan." So, this was the famous party-thrower extraordinaire. He wasn't bad looking. Nolan had light blonde hair which was styled in an off-centered part that was combed through with gel, making his hair curve off the right. He wore a white polo shirt with a red baggy sweater. Nolan pulled off the look just well enough so that he didn't look pretentious.

"Thanks. I'm Joey."

"I saw you from inside. You seemed lonely out here, and a pretty girl shouldn't be alone. That's why I brought you a drink."

"I'm not lonely. I'm just taking a breather. Does this have alcohol in it?" I asked, trying to be careful.

"Not a drop. I didn't know if you liked that type of stuff."

Nolan leaned over the railing, looking down at the forest as I drank my fruit punch.

When the cool liquid hit my lips, I realized I was thirstier than I had thought. Since it was only half a cup, I drank it till the last drop.

I'm pretty sure that was the moment where everything went all downhill.

CHAPTER 13
Drunk as a Skunk

"Are you okay?" a voice asked. It was a familiar voice, but I just couldn't determine it. I was so confused. All I saw was green. I didn't even know why it was just green everywhere.

"I'm fine," I tried to say to the person, but I wasn't even sure if I had actually said it or if I said it in my head.

"You don't look fine," the voice answered with amusement. So I guessed I had said it out loud. I still saw green everywhere. It just wouldn't go away. "I say this because you're hanging your arms over the railing, looking down at the grass."

Oh, so that's where the green came from. I swung my arms back and forth. I was, in fact, hanging over a railing. Don't even ask me why. I'm as confused as you are. I tried slowly to lift myself up, but I ended up tripping over my feet and landed on my butt.

"Are you okay?" the person asked again. This time, I could see the person's face. Still, I couldn't tell who it was. My vision swam, blurring all the colors together.

"Jesus?" I asked the mysterious man. I heard a soft chuckle.

"No, I'm not Jesus. I'm Nolan."

Oh, right, Nolan. He was there talking to me, and then I don't know what happened. Nolan bent down and scooped me up and held my body to his to keep me steady. "You stopped talking to me then started hanging over the rail."

"I don't know what's going on." Which was true. My mind felt scrambled. I couldn't think straight. My vision was blurry like how it is when I don't wear my glasses, but I was wearing them; I could feel them. My limbs felt as heavy as cinder blocks.

"You must have had too much to drink, is all," Nolan said with a laugh, shifting me in his arms. *But I didn't have anything to drink besides fruit punch.* That's what I wanted to say, but I couldn't get the words out.

I laid my head on Nolan's chest, not being able to keep it up. I would have thought this was uncomfortable since I just met him, but I couldn't think straight.

I then heard a low whistle, or at least I think I heard it. I could be imagining things now.

Along with the whistle, I heard footsteps coming toward us. "Man, she is totally gone." It's a girl's voice this time, and like the first one, the voice sounded familiar, but I just can't place it. "Thanks."

"No problem. Now time to get some action of my own. I don't know if she can stand though," Nolan spoke. His chest vibrated on my ear, making me giggle.

"Can you stand?" the girl's voice said with her lips close to my ear. I thought for a second. *Could I stand? Might as well try.*

I pushed myself off Nolan to stand upright. My legs wobbled only a little bit. I was proud to say that I could stand up straight. I grinned happily.

"See, I can stand all by myself," I slurred joyfully. I noticed that the girl speaking before was Danika.

"We can see that. Congrats," Danika said with amusement, and then she waved Nolan off. "I can take her from here."

Nolan just scoffed. Before heading inside the sliding doors, he turned and said, "You owe me." I wondered what she owed him for. Maybe she saved his puppy from drowning.

"Now…" Danika started turning her attention to me. "Let's go inside." I shrugged, going ahead of her, walking into the party confidently.

I continued walking with no set destination when someone collided with my shoulder harshly. "Watch where you're going, whore." The girl hissed. I was suddenly filled with anger.

I turned toward the girl, eyes flashing with anger. "And you look like a pumpkin, bitch!" I shouted before lunging at the girl.

Danika was quicker than I was because she put her arm around my waist. I struggled against her, still trying to get at the girl. I could hear Danika chuckling in my ear. The girl in front of us just glared before walking away.

I struggled against Danika again. "Yeah, that's right. Go back to your pumpkin patch!" I shouted after the girl. I could feel the rumble of Danika's laughter on my back.

"She didn't even look like a pumpkin," Danika said through her laughter. I didn't even know what she was laughing at. I looked around me, trying to find what was funny. I could only see large blobs of color, moving at a fast pace.

"Get off me," I said, pushing Danika away from me. I felt tired and sluggish. I didn't really have much energy after my outburst. I, with my head hanging, slowly walked over to a couch that was not occupied. I sat down with a big plop, slumping against the cushions. Danika followed me, sitting down right next to me. She put her arm around my shoulder, scooting closer, pressing her side against mine.

"Are you okay?" Everything felt like it was in slow motion. I clumsily scooted away from her into the couch arm. Danika smiled at me with her signature sultry smile. With hooded eyes, she moved next to me again, placing her hand on the couch arm, successfully trapping me between her body and the couch.

I swallowed the thick lump that was in my throat as Danika's cinnamon perfume enveloped me.

I pushed myself farther on the couch arm. "You don't look so good. Maybe I can help sober you up," Danika said, smiling a wicked grin.

She was right; I was no longer tired anymore. Danika kept leaning toward me. She lowered herself to my exposed neck, peppering the slope of my neck with kisses. I closed my eyes, trying to block everything out. Danika continued her path, trailing the kisses all the way up to the corner of my mouth.

She paused for a moment before leaning in, planting a hard kiss on my mouth. I yelped in surprise, pushing myself backward again. My glasses pressed into my nose as Danika tried continuing the kiss. I lifted my weak arms, putting my hands on her shoulders to push her off, but she was stronger.

Then someone lifted Danika off me, throwing her to the other side of the couch. "What the fuck!" my savior shouted. I still had my eyes closed, scared to look at Danika.

"Oh, come off it. We were just having a little fun. Upset because you weren't invited?" I didn't have to look at Danika to know that she had a smug look on her face.

"It didn't look like fun since you were forcing yourself on her." All their words began to blur together, and the couch seemed to come to life, rocking me back and forth.

I quickly got up, not wanting to be swallowed by its ravenous couch cushions. I stumbled a little bit into my savior. I immediately knew who my savior was once my body collided with theirs.

Her slender arms surrounded my body, holding me steady. I returned the action, putting my arms around her waist, burying my head into her shoulder, and taking a deep breath of mint and lilacs. I gave her one more tight squeeze before pulling back, standing on my own. I gave Olivia the biggest smile I could muster in my dizzy state.

Olivia returned it with an equally big smile, but then her mouth slowly turned into a frown. Olivia reached out, grabbing my chin. It wasn't as soft as the other times she had done it, but it still had an electrifying effect on me.

She clutched my chin while staring into my eyes. I happily stared back at Olivia, always happy to be given a chance to look at her warm brown eyes.

Olivia let go of my chin, storming over to Danika with clenched fists and nostrils flaring. I had no idea why she was so angry, but what I did know was that she looked gorgeous with anger radiating off her.

"Is she drunk?" Olivia hissed at Danika, who calmly crossed her legs looking up at Olivia.

"Just a little. But why does it matter? It's a party. You're supposed to get drunk."

Olivia flexed her hands and then started pacing in front of Danika. I didn't understand why Danika said I had a little when I only had fruit punch. Whatever. I was no longer concerned with Danika anymore. But I was interested in how smooth Olivia legs looked right now. I tilted my head to the side, trying to get a better look.

"Joey has never had alcohol before, and she clearly looked like she had more than a little," Olivia said, gesturing to me. I snapped my head up, but I had already been caught. Olivia looked like she wanted to smile, but she frowned again instead.

"I may have helped her along," Danika said nonchalantly, shrugging her shoulders, uninterested. Olivia whipped back to Danika with wide eyes.

"You what?" Olivia shouted. I was starting to get bored with them going back and forth over whatever, and I felt a little thirsty. I decided I would go and get something to drink. "This isn't a game, Danika. You can't just give someone alcohol and then sexually harass them!"

I walked away from them and went into the kitchen. When I walked in, a random guy slung his arm on my shoulder.

"You look thirsty." How did he know that? Mr. Random Guy must have been a psychic. "Care to do some body shots?"

I had no idea what body shots were. "If it involves me getting something to drink, then okay."

"Yes! That's the spirit!" The guy whooped loudly. "We got a taker!" He then shouted to everyone in the kitchen. People started to clear a counter to which the guy and I were dragged over to. The guy took off his shirt, flinging it into the crowd who were cheering "Shots!" repeatedly.

The random, now shirtless guy hopped up on the counter and lay flat on his back. Someone squeezed lime juice over his stomach then sprinkled salt on top. Someone passed me a tiny glass that looked like it was made for a doll. It was filled to the brim with what looked like water.

"Salt!" the crowd chanted over and over. I assumed I was supposed to eat the salt first. I had no idea why would salt go with water, but I guess it was a part of this entire game. So, I leaned over the guy's stomach, and in one clean swipe, I licked up the salt. The crowd went mad, jumping and shoving each other in all directions.

I finally could drink my water. Since the cup was so small, I drank it in one gulp. Strangely, it burned my throat when I swallowed it all. I coughed loudly, trying to get rid of the sensation.

The guy lifted himself off the counter. When his feet touched the floor, he did a little dance. Everyone shouted happily. I began to feel a little dizzy again, but I didn't have time to react to it before I was hoisted up and laid down on the counter. Someone came along and repeated the steps they did with the shirtless guy, but instead, they squeezed the lime near my cleavage since I was wearing a dress. The lime felt sticky against my skin.

After the salt was sprinkled, the random shirtless guy leaned in to lick it off. I cringed when his sandpaper tongue slowly lapped up the salt and lime from my neck.

"Oh, hell no!" I heard someone shout and thanked God for it because soon enough, the shirtless guy was pulled away from me. I was still lying down, so Olivia was at a slant. I giggled because she looked funny angry and slanted.

After Olivia pushed some of the crowd away from me, she came over, gently placing her hands on mine. She tugged me up from the counter. When I sat upright, I smiled again, happy to see her and not the shirtless guy.

"His tongue felt weird," I stated with all seriousness because it really did. I leaned into Olivia, still sitting on the counter. I press my nose to hers with a wolfish grin. "I bet yours tastes better," I whispered, deliberately breathing on her lips.

Olivia blinked a couple of times, staring at me. Then she stepped away from me, mumbling, "Oh God." She shook her head, staring at the floor. I could tell she had blush all over her cheeks. It felt good to make her blush.

"Let's get you out of here," Olivia said, putting an arm around my waist, helping me down from the counter. She still held my waist as we walked out of the kitchen together, which I was grateful for since I did feel wobbly.

When we got to Olivia's car, she leaned me against the car while she fished for her keys in her purse. I giggled loudly when I started sliding down the smooth car door surface. Olivia heard me laughing, so she looked up from her purse. She quickly caught me before I had slipped all the way to the ground.

"Where is Neal when I need him?"

I giggled again. Where was Neal? I had no idea. Maybe he was in the blob of color that was spreading in the house. "He is probably..." I stopped, trying to remember the word I wanted to use. "Fornicating?"

Olivia finally got her keys while holding me in her left arm. "I can't believe you just said fornicating." She laughed a little before opening the door of the car. Slowly, she struggled to get me into the car. When I was finally in, she pulled the seatbelt across my body.

Olivia closed the door then walked to the driver's side. I laid my head against the cool window, looking at the mess scattered on the lawn. My eyes felt heavy as I stare. I tried to fight to keep them open, but I couldn't. Even the rumble of the car engine didn't bring me from my sleep stupor.

~

My eyes opened when my head hit something hard. "Ow," I mumbled, lifting my hand to rub the sore spot.

"Oops. Sorry, Joey." Olivia apologized. "You're kinda heavy right now."

I realized we're walking up some stairs I had never seen before. Well, it was more like I was being dragged up the stairs. Olivia lifted me up carefully this time and took me into a room I had never been to before. Everything was dark and just looked like shapes, but I knew I had never been here before.

"I'm going to get you some clothes to wear," Olivia said as she laid me on the bed that was in the room. I sat there in the dark, not knowing what else to do but wait for her to come back. When she did, she had a pile of folded clothes with a toothbrush on the top.

"You can change into these." Olivia handed me the pile. There is a cute t-shirt on top with a funny looking T-Rex that said, *Rawr. It means I love you in dinosaur*, paired with some basketball shorts.

I put the clothes on the bed beside me. I then reached behind my back, dragging the zipper of my dress down. I tugged it over my head, then tossed it to the floor.

Olivia shrieked before covering her eyes and turning her back. "What are you doing?"

"I'm changing," I mumbled because I was tired and ready to pass out. I slowly put on the t-shirt and basketball shorts. "I'm done."

Olivia turned back at me with a grin and hands on her hips. "I meant to go to the bathroom and change."

"Too late." I shrugged.

Olivia sighed, shaking her head. "Get in the bed. I know you're tired."

I nodded. I was tired. I crawled over to the headboard, pulling the covers back, then got under them.

Olivia stood by me, leaning on the nightstand that was next to the bed. She just gazed at me with her brown eyes as I snuggled deeper into the covers. "Comfortable?"

I nodded, but strangely, I felt like something was missing. "Come here," I whispered.

Olivia curiously looked at me, but still, she bent down close to me. She hovered over me with a dazzling smile on her face. She reached out and tucked my blonde strands behind my ear. "What?"

I didn't even answer her question. I just stared back at her, loving the way the moon came in through the window and bathed the side of her face in white light. She looked so beautiful.

I propped myself up on my elbows, raising my face so it was level with hers. I leaned in and pressed a small kiss on the corner of her mouth. I heard a gasp come from Olivia's mouth. I pulled back a little just to see Olivia's face. She looked a little shocked; her brown eyes were a darker shade than before as she stared back at me.

I leaned in again, hovering on her mouth to see if she would react. When she didn't, I leaned in farther and pressed my lips softly against hers. Olivia seemed stunned at first, and then she quickly responded by moving her lips with mine.

My heartbeat sped up, drumming fast against my chest. I was no longer dazed as I felt before. Her lips were soft but

97

also urgent. My hands somehow found themselves tangled in her dark tresses. I swiped my tongue over her bottom lip, wanting more.

That's when Olivia pulled back. She stood back away from me with closed eyes and hands rubbing her temples. My whole body was buzzing, filled with the feeling of Olivia's lips on mine.

"Umm…" Olivia mumbled, trying to get her thoughts together. "I'm going to change." She walked over to the door, still looking at me on the way out. Her foot slammed into the door just as she was leaving. "Fuck." She groaned. I giggled watching her leave the room.

I laid back again, staring at the ceiling. I don't even know why I had just done that. I felt all weird right now anyways. Might as well top off the weirdness by kissing Olivia.

After the vibration in my body died down, I began to feel sleepy again. My eyes began to feel heavy even though I wanted to stay awake.

I know I remembered the bed dipping on the right side of me, but after that, I was passed out.

CHAPTER 14
Waking Up

I woke up with a massive headache. I didn't even want to open my eyes; it hurt so much. My mouth felt like it was filled with sand and cotton, which was an extremely gross feeling.

The only pleasant thing about waking up this morning was that I felt incredibly warm. I tried to bury myself deeper in the source of warmth. It was soothing to the pounding in my head.

Then I heard a groan; I froze my actions immediately. What the hell was I pressed against? I cracked my eyes open, but my vision was a little blurry. I tried lifting my arms to no avail since they were squished together on my chest. I blinked a couple of times, trying to clear my eyesight.

My vision cleared, but all I saw was smooth tan skin. Then I snapped my head upward, coming face to face with Olivia. Her long brown hair fell across her face, resting on the side of her lips. They were slightly parted, letting soft breaths escape.

I realized the reason I was being squished was that Olivia had her arms wrapped securely around my waist with hands locked together on the middle of my back.

I, Joey Montgomery, was in the same bed as Olivia Winchester. I was so shocked that I scrambled back out of her grasp. I didn't realize how close I was to the edge of the bed, so when I shot back, I tipped myself over the side of the bed. I tumbled to the floor with a loud bang.

Why did I have to be so inept?

Olivia sprung up from the bed when she heard the noise. She looked over the side of the bed with an amused grin. I really didn't pay much attention because I was rubbing my head to try to get it to stop pounding from the headache.

"Are you alright?" Olivia asked with a husky, sleep-coated voice. I almost forgot about how much my head hurt when I heard her voice; it sounded so hypnotizing. "Oh, you have a headache."

Olivia crawled out of bed quickly and went out the door. "I'll be right back." I was still on the floor when she came back with a glass filled to the brim with water and two capsules.

She set the water and capsules down carefully on her nightstand, then Olivia put two hands out for me to take. I reached up and grabbed her hands. She slowly pulled me up, trying not to cause me any more pain than I needed. Olivia set me down on the edge of her bed, and then she passed me the water and capsules.

Olivia bent down in front of me, placing her hands on my knees. "It's ibuprofen. It will help with your headache." I took the pills as soon as she said that, drinking all the water to the last drop.

"You're still clumsy when you're not even fully awake yet," Olivia commented with a soft smile.

I smiled back at her, rubbing my face, and I realized that I still had my glasses on. It's surprising that I didn't break them in my sleep. Her palms on my knees felt warm through my too long basketball shorts. "It's kinda my thing."

"That it is." Olivia's smile widened.

We sat in silence for a few moments with Olivia staring at me with her sparkling eyes and dazzling smile while I tried to avoid her eye contact, drawing lazy circles in her covers.

"Last night, Danika and Nolan had spiked your drink."

I nodded, figuring that is what had happened. Anger stirred within me. I couldn't believe that Danika would stoop so

100

low and take advantage of me. And for what? Whatever rivalry was going on between her and Olivia, it was despicable.

We sat in silence again, not really knowing what to say. After a while, Olivia spoke.

"Can I ask you a question?" Olivia said, taking her eyes off me and staring at the floor with a light blush coating her cheeks.

"Sure."

Olivia waited a long moment; it looked like she was gathering herself. "Do you remember last night?"

Of course, she would ask that. I remembered going to the party with Neal, Gwen, and Olivia. Olivia went dancing with lackey 1 and 2. Then there was Nolan and Danika. After that, I'm not too sure what had happened. For some reason, I kept seeing someone's stomach, which was weird.

Then I remembered something else. Olivia and I had kissed. I kissed Olivia.

I paused for a moment, trying to get my thoughts together. I cleared my throat before speaking. "Yes, I do."

Olivia pursed her lips together, looking at the floor, blush still spreading all the way to her ears. "Do you...do you regret it?"

I looked directly at her face, this time gazing at her features. She looked nervous about what I might say as an answer.

As I looked at Olivia's nervous and beautiful face, my heart sped up just a little. I wanted to smile just looking at the cute blush that adorned her face. Butterflies racked my stomach just thinking about when a smile is on her face rather than the blush. I didn't regret kissing her.

I regret the party maybe, but not kissing her.

"No, I don't."

Olivia sighed heavily, and her shoulder slumped with relief. "Good, but I don't want our relationship to be based off

101

some drunken kiss. Don't get me wrong. It was pretty amazing, but I want us to be different."

I nodded in understanding.

Olivia ran her hand through her long, brown, unkempt hair. "So now that is settled, I do want to start something here." She straightened her back and held her chin up with confidence. "Will you go on a date with me?"

My jaw slackened. I was so shocked whereas I couldn't speak for a few moments. "D-did you j-just ask me on a d-date?" I squeaked.

Olivia chuckled, lightly running her hand over the back of her neck and standing up from where she was still bent in front of me. "Yes."

I cleared my throat again before speaking. "What would you say if I said I will think about it?"

Olivia smiled widely. "I would say I'll take what I can get." She put her hands on her hips, sighing heavily. "Feels nice to get that off my chest, and now I'm going to make you breakfast." She smiled at me again before leaving the room.

Olivia's head popped in a few seconds later. "You can use the shower if you want; fresh towels and everything. I left your dress hanging in the bathroom." With a quick smile, she left for good this time.

I did as instructed. With sloth-like movements, I moved toward the bathroom to shower. And no, I was not going to dwell on the fact that I was using that same shower that Olivia used. Nope, not one bit.

I quickly showered and dried off, then I got dressed. I couldn't find the toothbrush I was given last night, so I just took some toothpaste and put it in my mouth. My hair was still wet from the shower, so I put it in a messy braid. I put my glasses back on my face and grabbed my phone, then headed into the hall.

Still feeling some of the effects of my headache, I trudged my out of the bathroom and made my way to the stairs.

102

I paused at the top of the stairs when I heard voices coming from the kitchen.

"So, who is this girl? Come on. You never make breakfast for your one-nights," I heard an unfamiliar girl voice speak from downstairs.

"Will you keep it down? She might hear you. I'm just making her breakfast," Olivia said to the other person. I didn't even know there was someone else in the house.

"Fine, but I'm just pointing out the obvious here."

"I don't need you to point out anything, especially when she comes down," Olivia said with annoyance.

I took that as my cue since I really didn't want to stand here forever; it kind of felt like I was eavesdropping (probably because I was). I made my way down the stairs slowly, making sure I didn't trip because that would not be a good first impression to whomever Olivia was talking to.

I walked into the kitchen with my head tilted downward, then I sat on a chair away from the girl. When I heard a low whistle, I pulled my head upward, looking at the other girl in the room.

The girl was small, sitting at the island bar in the kitchen with her feet dangling in her stool. She looked about thirteen or so. She had long brown hair that went to her hips and hazel eyes that were a mixture of brown and green. The girl had a wide smile as she looked at me up and down.

"Now I know why you're cooking breakfast 'cause she is totally hot," the girl said, looking at Olivia with a mocking smile.

Olivia rolled her eyes and brought a plate of food over to me. It was filled with small portions of eggs, bacon, and toast.

"Thank you," I said, finding it cute that she made breakfast for me. She returned it with an equally adorable, shy smile.

Olivia cleared her throat, blush spreading across her face. "Joey, this is my little sister, Ellie. Ellie, this is Joey," Olivia said, giving Ellie a pointed look, which they thought I missed, but I saw it. Ellie nodded quickly with understanding then went back to shoveling food in her mouth.

I paused from eating my food. I smiled at Ellie then said, "Nice to meet you."

Ellie stopped eating as well. She looked at me with shock written all over her face. "Wait a second. She is hot and nice! Usually, everyone just ignores me!" Ellie reached over and patted Olivia on the shoulder, who brushed her hand off. I kept my head low while eating, not wanting them to see me blush.

"Ellie, stop it."

"I'm just saying."

"Whatever," Olivia said, glaring at her sister who stared back head on. My phone vibrated, causing them to look away from each other and stare at me.

I looked down to see who was texting me. I knew it could only be one person since only one person actually texts me.

Are you okay? We need to talk. Can you come over? Neal said in his text. I forgot all about him due to the party last night and the presence of Olivia. I did need to see him because we really did need to talk.

I'm great actually. I'll come over in a little while.

I looked up from my phone to find Olivia looking at me with a perfect eyebrow arched, wondering who had texted me.

"I have to go."

Olivia's mouth turned into a frown as soon as I said that.

I smiled a little, knowing she wanted me to stay. "Neal is worried about me."

Olivia nodded in understanding. She took all our plates away and put them in the sink. "I'll walk you out."

I hopped off the stool and walked to toward the doorway. I turned to Ellie before leaving. "Again, nice meeting you, Ellie."

"You too." Ellie nodded at me.

Olivia smiled, putting her hand lightly on my back and leading me to the doorway. She opened the door for me. I walked out the door, but I was stopped when she grabbed my wrist.

"Before you leave..." She pulled her hand away. "I wanted to say I am sorry for leaving you at the party by yourself," Olivia said, hanging her head in shame, scuffing her foot against the sidewalk.

"It's not your fault. You didn't know that was going to happen," I said, trying to ease her guilt.

"Still—"

"No, it wasn't your fault. It was Danika and Nolan's."

"She could have taken it much further than she did and you could have gotten hurt. I wasn't there for you!" Olivia exclaimed with tears in her eyes. I stepped up toward her boldly and put my arms around her waist, pulling her into a hug. She returned it slowly, putting her arms around my neck.

"But I didn't," I said with my head lying on her shoulder.

With one more squeeze, Olivia broke the hug, stepping back from me and wiping her face where tears had escaped. She looked at the ground shyly then.

"Do you think I can have your phone number?"

I gaped at her. I couldn't believe she just asked for my number. First, the date thing, and now this.

"Y-yes. Give me your phone," I said, passing her my phone. She pulled out hers and passed it to me. I typed my number in her phone then handed it back to her as she did the same.

"Bye then," Olivia said. She leaned forward and kissed me on the corner of my mouth. I flushed a light red and smiled at her shyly.

"Bye," I whispered to her. Olivia grabbed my hand and gave me a bright smile.

"Bye."

"Bye."

"Bye."

"Oh my gosh!" Ellie shouted from inside the house. "You guys are nauseating."

Olivia laughed at her sister's comment, and I couldn't help but laugh along with her. "I'll see you later then."

"Yeah," Olivia said, rubbing her neck, which she seemed to do when she was nervous. "Don't forget to text me."

"I won't." I waved before finally taking my leave from her house. Neal and I sure did have a lot to talk about.

CHAPTER 15
Little Talks

I decided to go to my house before going to Neal's. I walked the whole way because no one's house was too far away from each other's in this neighborhood and I needed time to clear my head before speaking with Neal.

When I got there, my sister's car was the only one parked in the driveway.

I cringed as soon as I saw it. I had disappeared last night, not even bothering to call home. It wasn't for my parent's sake but more for my sister's. My parents probably didn't even know I had gone to the party. I knew she cared about my wellbeing.

I hesitated before I walked into the house, slowly closing the door, trying not to make my presence known to my sister. Then I tiptoed to the stairs.

I didn't get a foot up on a step before I heard Gwen growl from behind me. "Where in the hell have you been?" she snapped.

I cringed for the second time, slowly swiveling around to face her. "I-I was uh…" Good thing Gwen started ranting before I could even finish.

"I was worried when I couldn't find you when we were leaving the party," she shouted, throwing her hands up in frustration. "I called you about a hundred times. I thought something had happened to you."

I really should have checked my messages. I hung my head with guilt, not really wanting to look at her face that was filled with disappointment. "I-I'm sorry."

Gwen sighed loudly, putting her hands on her hips, tilting her head toward the ceiling. "It's alright. It's just that you have never been to a party before, and I shouldn't have left you."

"It was expected." As soon as the words left my mouth, I felt kind of bad; Gwen's lips turned into a frown. Gwen felt bad when I brought up the fact that I'm always at home alone or our parents really don't care about me that much because she often tried to ignore it. "I m-mean, it was a party. I expected you to go off and have fun." I didn't expect her to take Neal with her.

Gwen looked at me with an unreadable expression before coming over to me and pulling me into a hug. I haven't gotten a hug from Gwen since I was at least 10 or so. I was so shocked I just stood there as she hugged me. I felt like I was being rude not returning it, so I lifted a hand and patted her awkwardly on the back.

"So, what really happened? Where were you?"

I didn't want to tell her that Nolan had spiked my drink, or about what Danika had done, or the fact that Olivia had left me alone for a few moments because then, all hell would break loose. So, I thought on my feet.

"Uh, w-well Olivia had a f-few drinks, and I didn't think it was safe f-for her to drive home, so I-I took her." I swallowed trying to keep my stutter in check otherwise she would surely know I was lying. "Then Olivia let me stay at her house." I sort of mumbled the last part, but she still heard me.

"Are you serious?" Gwen said with squinted eyes and a big Cheshire-type grin. I ducked my head trying to hide my blush, looking down at my feet. "Did something happen?" I just stood there, not saying anything, trying to avoid the question.

I was released from my misery when we heard someone come lumbering down the stairs. My grandma came down lugging to suitcases. I rushed forward to help rest of the way.

"Thank you, kangaroo," she said, a little breathless while making her way down the rest of the stairs. "Let's get this show on the road; I don't want to miss my flight."

My shoulders slumped immediately when I heard that. I had completely forgotten this was grandma's last day here. She would be leaving me to the wolves that were my parents. Without her, judgment would come at me in heaps.

"Sure thing," Gwen said giving me one last look, then scooped up grandma's suitcases and took them outside to her car.

"Goodbye, grandma," I said dejectedly, not directly looking at her. It was always like this when she left, we didn't hang out much, but she made me feel safe.

"Kangaroo, don't be sad. There will always be next time." She literally always said that when she leaves. It was the same routine. I get all teary-eyed, and then grandma says she will be back. I nodded, and in my head, I think that she will be back, but it's never soon enough.

"I know."

Grandma gave me a sad smile before coming over to me and wrapped me in a hug. I returned it automatically. She ruffled my hair then released me. With a small wave, grandma left.

I let out a small sigh then trudged my way up the stairs to my room to change out of this dress then head over to Neal's.

~

I knocked softly on Neal's front door then waited with my hands clasped behind my back. Ms. Ramsey swung open the door not a minute later with a huge smile on her face.

"Josephine, honey, I haven't seen you in so long!" Ms. Ramsey exclaimed, pushing her red locks out of her freckled face and stepped aside.

"I saw you at the mixer," I said with a broad smile and a nonchalant wave of the hand. I walked past her and into the house. I was just about to go up the stairs when Ms. Ramsey spoke again.

"Before you go, I bought you and Neal some goodies. Wait here." She left the room and went into the kitchen while I bounced on my toes excited for the candy I was about to get.

Ms. Ramsey came back holding bags of gummy bears (my personal favorite), Twizzlers, and Starburst jelly beans. Why did she want to kill me? I went over to her, taking the bags out of her arms then leaned over to kiss her on the cheek.

"Thank you!" I squealed with excitement.

"You're welcome. Don't you dare eat all of it, save some for later?" she said with a scolding finger. I laughed, going up the stairs not promising anything.

I turned left and went straight to Neal's bedroom door. I didn't even bother knocking because what was his was mine.

Neal was stretched out on his bed, reading something called *Gifted Hands* by Ben Carson. I chuckled when I saw his t-shirt. It said, "Never trust an atom…They make up everything." It was such a corny joke, but hilarious at the same time.

When he just continued reading, failing to notice my presence, I huffed and went over to him. I snatched the book out his hand then tossed it on his desk.

"Hey! I was reading—" Neal stopped talking mid-sentence when I dumped that candy on his lap. He stared at it with wide eyes. "Where did you get this gold mine?" he asked as he ripped out the bag of Twizzlers, sticking a couple in his mouth.

"Your mom gave them to me." I took a couple out of the bag as well, putting them in my mouth, making them look like a walrus' teeth.

He snatched them from my teeth and then tossed them at my face. I laughed, tossing them back, then his face turned somber.

"I'm sorry I left you at the party. It was stupid of me. I was pretty worried. So was Gwen." It felt like everyone was apologizing to me because I was happy to see that they cared about me.

"It's okay. You aren't my babysitter, you know."

"Yeah, I get that, but I just wanted to say I'm sorry."

I tossed another Twizzler at him, which he quickly stuffed into his mouth. "Apology accepted."

"Ready to get everything that's in your mind off your chest?" Neal said with a mouth full of Twizzlers, and he told me not to talk with food in my mouth.

I shook my head no. I don't think I was ready to confront my feelings, and not just because I began to feel nauseous, more because I was terrified that if I said it out loud, it would be real and I would have to face it.

"Well, you're going to tell me anyway, and I'll tell you what's been happening to me lately as well."

I nodded, watching Neal as he swiped the candy onto the floor then lied down next to it on his back. I followed suit lying on my back next to him with the candy in the middle.

We usually did this when things got little hectic, or new situations happened that caused us to think more than usual, so we get together to lie on our backs and talk out our problems; we trusted each other. It felt like the troubles of life were more bearable lying down, it was like it made the earth stop spinning for just a moment so you can catch up.

"Want me to go first?" Neal asked, tilting his head to the side to look at me. I nodded.

Neal took a deep breath before speaking. "It was about the summer before this school year. You weren't home that day, I think you went to visit your grandmother, and I didn't know about it. Anyways, I came over, and Gwen was home. I was

111

going to leave, but your sister invited me to eat dinner with her. I said yes." He paused, looking at me for my reaction. When I didn't say anything, he continued with his story. "One thing leads to another, I guess, and now we have been dating for about a week."

We sat in silence for a couple of moments. Neal chewed nervously on a Twizzler, waiting for me to speak. Instead, I opened the bag of gummy bears then stuffed a fist-full in my mouth. I chewed slowly, trying to think of what to say.

"Why didn't you tell me?"

"We thought you would be angry," he answered. "But recently, we got tired of sneaking around and whatnot. We felt like you should know. Are you mad?"

"I'm not mad, I'm just a little hurt that you didn't tell me, but I understand why you didn't."

"It's not that I don't trust you. It was just that we didn't know how you would feel about your best friend dating your sister," Neal said with a small chuckle. I guess I should have been mad, but I wasn't. If they wanted to be together, who was I to stop them?

"Well, I'm happy for you two. Really." He grinned to which I grinned back.

"Good, now your turn," he said, reaching over to get some gummy bears.

I took a deep breath, chewing on my lip nervously. My face heated all the way to the tips of my ears. I twiddled with a red gummy bear that I still had not eaten yet; I like to save those for last. I put my hands over my face, not wanting to see his reaction. "Olivia asked me on a date," I whispered.

Neal shot up from his spot, sitting up straight, with eyes wide. "You're shitting me?" I laughed a little, which came out muffled under my hands.

"No, I'm not shitting you. She asked me this morning."

"Wait, hold on!" Neal said with eyes almost falling out his sockets. "What happened to you at the party?"

I wanted to feed him the same lies that I did with my sister, but I trust him, though I don't want him going on some type of protective rampage. I still didn't want to lie, so I modified the story a bit. "Danika got me a little drunk last night." Neal looked so angry that I could practically see the steam coming out his ears. I sat up, and I patted his arm to try to calm him down. "Olivia handled it. I wasn't, uh, put together enough to go home on my own, so she took me to her place."

"Wow. Now, I feel even worse for leaving you," he said. I just nodded my head, already over it. Then Neal's eyebrows shot up to his forehead. "You slept over at her house?!" I blushed, lying hard on my back with a thud, covering my face again. "Oh my gosh! You didn't just sleep over at her house, you slept in her bed!" I blushed even harder; I couldn't cover my embarrassment any longer. I quickly crawled up on Neal's bed and dived under his blankets.

Neal laughed loudly, dropping all his candies on the floor and jumped on top of me, bouncing up and down. "I can't believe this!" Neal shouted, ripping the cover away from my face. "You slept in the same bed as Olivia freaking Winchester!" he exclaimed right in my face.

I cringed a bit, knowing since I already told him the beginning of the story, mind as well tell him the rest. "I also k-kissed her," I said quickly, tearing off the Band-Aid. Neal stopped bouncing immediately. His mouth fell open as he stared at me.

"You what?!"

Apparently, his mind couldn't take the shock. "I kissed Olivia." Neal just sat on top off me, staring. "I was drunk. And her lips looked soft," I mumbled the last part, but the way his eyes looked right about now, I'm pretty sure he heard me.

Neal crawled off me and leans on the headboard of the bed. I pushed myself up and sat next to him, "So you like her?"

"I think I do," I said truthfully. I think I did like her. If butterflies in my stomach, blush on my face, and the rapid

113

heartbeat I got when she was near meant that I like her, then I'm pretty sure I did.

"Do you even like girls?"

"I like this one." I never really thought about my sexuality and I wasn't sure what this meant for me, but I knew that I liked Olivia. She had a confidence that I just couldn't help but admire, along with such a magnetic personality, it was just hard not to like her. She was sweet to me, and I have never had that before. I had previously considered that maybe it was just because no one had ever shown me attention, but waking up this morning with her, I knew that wasn't the case at all. It was Olivia that I liked.

"Did you say yes to the date?" Neal said, before reaching over me to grab the jelly beans that were on the floor. I laughed at how silly he looked with his long thin arms stretching out towards the candy. He came back up with the bag, taking a fist full. He put some in his mouth then put some up to mine; I took them willingly.

"No, I told her I would think about it. She gave me her number though."

Neal chuckled, popping more jelly beans in his mouth while giving me a sideways look. "You sly dog."

I laughed along with him. "What should I tell her?"

"Clearly, you like her, so tell her yes."

I sighed, I really did want to say yes, but there was something holding me back. "What about my mother?" I had no idea what happens if Olivia and I were together. I blushed just thinking about it. I didn't care about everyone else, just my mother really. This would give my mother another reason to think I was a failure.

Neal slammed the bag of jelly beans on the bed, causing some jelly beans to escape and jump around on the covers. "May I be frank?" he asked, staring at me with seriousness all over his face. When I didn't respond, he continued. "Fuck your mother. You deserve to be happy."

I leaned over and buried my face in Neal's scrawny chest; he circled his arm around my back in response. He was right, I should not care about what my mother would think; I should just be happy with myself. Olivia made me happy.

I pulled out my phone, enjoying the sound of Neal chewing in my ear for some weird reason as I typed out a simple message to Olivia.

"Yes."

CHAPTER 16
Cotton Candy

To say the least, I was freaking out.

Olivia and I had decided that we would meet this upcoming Saturday. The entire school week was filled with me trying to dodge Olivia's heated stares and warm smiles. Shy glances were often shared between us whenever we were in the same room.

We didn't have much of a chance to talk with each other though, due to Olivia having student council meetings like crazy, regular class time, and her parents always dragged her to whatever event they had planned. But Olivia still found time to find me in the school halls and grip my hand softly before darting away to class. Her impromptu contact always left me a blushing, stammering mess.

After a long wait, it was finally Saturday, and I was freaking out in front of my full-length mirror, not having any idea what to wear on our date. I got massive nervous and excited butterflies in my stomach every time I thought of the fact that I was going on a date with Olivia.

My mother had already returned all my clothes, now that my grandma was no longer here, but now I wish she hadn't. Everything I picked in my closet just didn't look right; it all felt too underdressed. It felt weird to me. I had almost forgotten what it was like to dress like myself. God, I had missed it.

I ran back to my walk-in closet for the hundredth time, throwing off my clothes and trying on something new. My speed changes were causing my entire room to look like a hurricane had hit. Clothes and shoes were tossed all around the room in random places. It was no use.

I would never find anything in my closet suitable for my date with Olivia, but I refused to wear those circus outfits my mother had in my closet before. All my clothes looked like I was a lazy bum. I could only think of one person who could help in this situation.

"Gwen!" I shouted from inside my closet. When she didn't come a few seconds later, I shouted again. "Gwen!"

"I'm coming!" I could hear Gwen's voice from outside the closet. I hurried out, tripping over a shoe in the process. Luckily, I managed not to face-plant on my carpet floor.

"Whoa, where's the fire?" Gwen said, smirking when she saw me trip. I scratched my cheek in embarrassment and then held my hands behind my back sheepishly.

"I, uh, need a favor."

Gwen crossed her arms over her chest with a smug grin. "You need my help?"

I sighed loudly, exasperated. "Yes, I need your help, and I don't have time for you to rub it in. Olivia is coming to pick me up in about an hour for—" I paused for a moment, looking away from Gwen "—our date."

Gwen's mouth then formed an 'o' as she stared at me. "A what?"

"Gwen!" I whined, sounding like a three-year-old. But I didn't care, this was urgent. "I don't have time for this. Will you help me? I can't find an outfit."

"As much as I want to milk the fact that you are going on a date with Olivia, I will move past it because you look desperate. I will help, on one condition."

I groaned out loud again; of course, she would want something. "Fine."

"You have to tell me all the details of your date."

"That's it?"

"Yep, that's it." Gwen grinned before walking over to the door, leaving and faintly said, "I'll be back."

She came back quickly with an armful of her clothes. Gwen tossed them on my bed and began to make outfits with them. "Pick which one you want."

All the outfits she had picked consisted of skirts, dresses, and tons of frilly shirts. None of them really seemed like me though. And I wanted to just be me again. No more frilly high society. I reached out and picked up an off-white Rolling stones crop top. It didn't seem that bad.

"This is cool." I didn't really like anything else. Gwen could see that I didn't by the look on my face. So with a sigh, she walked in my closet. She came out with a pair of my beat-up combat boots and some plain old skinny jeans.

I put the outfit on quickly, the rushed to look in the mirror. The outfit was like me with a dash of Gwen. I didn't look half bad. A little of my stomach was showing, but it wasn't a lot. I tucked my jeans into my boots.

"Do you want those contacts back?" Gwen said while perching herself on my desk; the desk squeaked when she shifted her weight.

"No, I think I'll just stick with my glasses," I said, pushing them back up the bridge of my nose. I was comfortable with my glasses. My hair was just styled with an off-centered part, causing most of my hair to go to one side of my face. "How do I look?" I said, sticking my arms out so Gwen could get a look at the full outfit.

Gwen cocked her head to the side, looking at me up and down. "Not bad."

"Good," I said, going back to the mirror to check how I looked once more. From outside the house, I could hear Olivia's car horn honk. I whipped around and looked at my sister with eyes wide. "Oh god, she is here! What do I do?"

Gwen chuckled at my nervousness. She hopped off the desk gracefully, coming over to stand in front of me. "You go

118

have fun, duh." Gwen put her hands on my shoulders in a comforting way.

"Thanks," I said with my voice full of sincerity.

"No problem." Gwen squeezed my shoulder one more time. Then with a cheeky smile, she said, "I think I'll go call Neal."

"Gross." I smiled back, giving her a hint that I was joking. Gwen smiled even wider, before exiting my room.

I let out a huge sigh, trying to get my nerves under control before I saw Olivia. "I can do this," I said giving myself a mini pep talk before trotting out my room and down the stairs.

When I opened the front door and went down the steps, I could see Olivia leaning on the passenger side door, waiting for me. She looked beautiful in simple a black v-neck and white cut off shorts. Olivia had a warm smile on her face as she watched me walk toward her.

"Hi," Olivia greeted when I stood in front of her.

"Hi," I said, tucking a strand of hair behind my ear, realizing that my little pep talk didn't do squat, now that I was standing in front of her. I was nervous as hell.

"Ready?"

I nodded, not trusting my voice. Olivia just gave me a lopsided smile before opening the car door for me. I slid into the seat quickly, allowing her to shut the door behind me. Olivia walked around the car before getting in on her side.

As I reached over to pull my seatbelt, I could see, out the corner of my eye, Olivia looking at my stomach as my shirt rose a little. I guess the shirt wasn't such a bad idea after all.

"You like nice."

"A-are you saying that you don't like it when I look like Malibu Barbie?"

"I'm not saying that I don't, because I really do," Olivia said with a light blush on her cheeks. "I just like it when you dress like you."

119

I smiled shyly, looking out the window instead of her gaze. "So where are you taking me?"

"It's a surprise."

~

Finally, after at least a thirty-minute drive, we pulled into the parking lot of a carnival. I stared at Olivia with inquisitive eyes while she giddily wiggled in her seat.

"Surprise! It's a carnival!" Olivia said happily. I still didn't understand what the big deal was. Olivia sighed when she realized I still didn't get it. "It's the place where we had our first kiss." She clarified with a heavy blush on her face.

I ducked my head in embarrassment, but I had a wide smile none the less. This was probably the sweetest thing anyone has ever done for me, and I didn't even pick up on it.

"But this time, we get to actually have fun rather than work." I nodded in agreement. This would be much better than working all day in the hot sun. Olivia unbuckled her seat belt and was about to exit the car before she said, "Oh, and no kissing booths."

I smiled even wider when Olivia showed her possessiveness. Lucky for her, I didn't want Olivia kissing anybody else either.

"Let's go!" Olivia squealed, finally getting out the car. I unbuckled my seatbelt, ready to open the door, only to find Olivia opening it for me. I already knew she would be doing that all day. I smiled at her as a silent thank you.

As we walked toward the park, I paid no attention to the rides looming over us, the kids shouting in excitement, or the varied of smells that ranged from delicious greasy food to an animal farm, only because Olivia took the liberty of slipping her hand into mine, intertwining our fingers. Every time she gripped my hand a little tighter, my heart raced just a little bit more.

I couldn't even focus what on what was going on around me. I could only focus on her.

120

"Let's get on that!" Olivia said with sheer excitement, and after that, the rest was history. I wasn't a real roller coaster person, but as soon as Olivia looked at me with her big brown eyes, I couldn't help but melt. I went along with every single thing she had planned for us.

We went on ride after ride, filled with Olivia clutching my hand on each ride. I knew it wasn't because she was scared; it was mostly because we wanted to keep contact with each other.

This was hands down probably the best day of my life.

As we were walking, we tried to look at everything that we passed by. Children ran all around us in excitement with their parents trailing tiredly behind them, trying to keep up. You can also see couples occasionally passing by. I'd like to think that for everyone looking at us, we were just a normal couple too. Me and Olivia. A couple.

I was so engrossed in the atmosphere that I almost didn't notice Olivia's gaze linger on a medium-sized white bunny with big floppy ears and a red bowtie that was hanging at one of the game booths. I could tell she wanted it, so I let go of her hand and went off to the booth which was called Shoot 'Em Up Ducks.

"What are the rules?" I asked the teen that was working at the booth just as Olivia jogged up behind me. She looked like she was about to protest, but I just smiled at her, letting her know that I was going to try to get that bunny no matter what she said.

He wiped his curly brown locks off his sweaty forehead before saying, "It's pretty easy. All you got to do is hit the ducks that pop up when the buzzer starts."

I pointed up to the bunny, holding my arm in place so he would know which one I was talking about. "How many do I have to hit for that one?"

The guy cleared his throat, openly leering at my stomach as my shirt rose. I wouldn't have worn the shirt if I had known other people besides Olivia would have been looking at my torso. Olivia, noticing the guy's eyes moving downward, grabbed my hand and gave a pointed glare at the booth guy.

He cleared his throat again before speaking. "You just got to hit six before the timer runs out."

It sounded easy enough. I was pretty sure I could do it since I have played shooting games for countless hours with Neal. I hand the guy three dollars like the sign said. When he pressed the buzzer, moving ducks popped up from behind a wooden barricade with red bull eyes on them. I instantly started shooting, hitting three. Olivia was jumping up and down behind me excitedly, shouting words of encouragement. I struck two more before the clock started winding down. When the timer hit the number two, I was finally able to beat the last duck.

Olivia squealed behind me, jumping over to me, wrapping me in a hug. Then she leaned forward and kissed me on the cheek. All I could do was smile widely and try not to pass out.

The guy went over with a stick and grabbed the bunny, handing it to Olivia with a red face, refusing to look us in the eye.

We walked off holding hands once again and Olivia clutching the bunny tightly.

"Thanks, Joey."

"No problem," I said giving her a smile.

We continued through the park until our stomach started growling. Olivia immediately dragged me over to the concession stands the carnival had lined up. She picked out two corn dogs, fries, and a bag of cotton candy to share. When I went in my pocket to pay, Olivia waved me off with a simple. "I got it."

After we paid, we went and sat on a bench near a carousel, with her bunny on her side. Sadly, we had to let go of each other's hands to eat. Easy conversation flowed between us as we ate; there was hardly ever an awkward silence. Olivia tried to feed me fries a couple of times, but I refused because I didn't want to look like a baby in front of everyone in the park. Then she stared at me with big brown sad eyes, and I relented, which left her in a fit of giggles.

Just after we finished, Olivia went to throw our wrappers away then opened the giant bag of cotton candy.

Immediately, I stuck my hand in and grabbed a handful of the pink sugary temptation. Olivia laughed at my gusto, knowing my problem with sweets which was probably her reason for buying it. I stuffed a handful of cotton candy in my mouth, loving the way it just melted on my tongue.

Olivia then stopped eating her portions and pointed to the side of my mouth. Her mouth was full; she couldn't speak, so I assumed cotton candy still stuck on my mouth. I tried to get it off, but I clearly was unsuccessful because Olivia kept laughing at me.

She scooted closer to me. I thought she was going to wipe it off like any other person would do, but instead, she put her lips directly on mine. I almost dropped the bag of cotton candy; I was so surprised. The feeling of her soft, perfect lips on mine made me light-headed. The cotton candy instantly melted between us, making the kiss even sweeter than it already was. It was short and gentle, but I felt it all through my body.

When she pulled away, she simply said, "All gone." with a suggestive smile. My entire body was invaded with a sensation I could only describe as electrifying. A dopey smile appeared on my face as I sat, staring at her in awe. Olivia always seemed to never stop surprising me.

"Come on, let's get on a couple more rides before the sun sets," Olivia said, grabbing my hand again and pulling me up from where I sat. I followed willingly behind her, and I knew then that I would go to the ends of the earth for this girl.

123

CHAPTER 17
The Changes That Make Us

The ride to my house was soothing even though some of the left-over excitement was still vibrating in our bodies. I had my head laid back on the headrest, comfortable with just watching Olivia drive. Olivia made it even better by humming the parts of the song that was playing. She wasn't even bothered by that fact that I was staring at her. We still hadn't let go of each other's hands; only doing so when it was necessary.

A small smile appeared on Olivia's face when I would pull her hand closer to me. I just had the urge to be near her, glad to be able to hold her hand in mine for as long as I wanted without any protest.

I was so focused on the circles I was making in the palm of Olivia's hand that I didn't even know the car had stopped in front of my house.

Olivia didn't say anything, just letting me continue making imaginary paths in her hand. I wasn't ready to leave her just yet.

Olivia clearly wasn't either because she made no moves to stop me. "Did you have fun?" she questioned, breaking the serene silence.

"I really did," I answered earnestly.

"Good. I'm glad you did. I was nervous about the whole carnival thing," Olivia said sheepishly, staring at our conjoined hands.

My mouth fell open just a little bit. "You were nervous?"

"Yes," she answered simply. I couldn't believe that the ever so confident Olivia was nervous about being with me.

"I really like you." And once again I was speechless. She admitted to being nervous and liking me all in the same sitting. A smile broke out over my face. I couldn't really help it. The first person that I have ever liked, who was way out of my league I might add, felt the same toward me.

"I really like you too." A smile that matched mine was on Olivia's face too. We sat there, staring at each other with identical smiles.

I couldn't help but let my eyes fall to Olivia's plump pink lips. I really wanted to kiss her then, but I didn't want to come off as too forward. But regardless of what my brain was thinking, my body gravitated forward. We were so close that each little breath Olivia took fell on my lips. Her eyes closed as she waited for me to make the next move.

Fuck it.

I closed the gap between us eagerly, pressing my lips to Olivia's. The kiss ignited every nerve ending in my body and only intensified when Olivia reached up and place her hands at the base of my jaw, holding me in place. Her tongue slid through my parted lips, deepening the kiss. I couldn't help but feel a little lightheaded as Olivia's tongue moved against mine.

I don't know how long we had kissed, but when we had finally parted, our chests were heaving up and down, trying to get air back into our lungs.

I have never been kissed like that. I had only been kissed once or twice back when everyone I knew didn't think that there was something wrong with me. But neither compared to Olivia's kisses. I really didn't want to go now, not after a kiss like that.

Olivia stared at me, mouth opened with a light blush on her face. I think she was just as surprised as I was.

A car revved past, breaking the spell that we were both under, pulling us back into reality.

"I guess I have to go now."

She didn't say anything, electing just to stare at me, eyes sparkling with mirth. "Do you want me to walk you to the door?"

Honestly, I would have loved for Olivia to walk me to the door, but I didn't want Gwen to see if Olivia tried to kiss me again. Gwen would never let me live it down.

"No, I'm okay," I said while unbuckling my seat belt.

"Okay then. Bye."

"Bye."

"Bye."

"Bye." Olivia looked like she was going to bid me farewell again, but with some surprising confidence, I leaned over and peck her own the lips as a final goodbye. When I pulled away, Olivia had a reddish hue to her face, surprise evident in her eyes.

"I really got to go," I said sadly, opening my door and stepping out. When I closed the door, I could hear Olivia call out.

"I'll text you." I nodded and smiled at her through the window. As I walked to the door, Olivia still sat on the curb, watching me. When I opened the door with my key, I turned back and waved at Olivia. She waved back eagerly before pulling off.

I walked into the house with a big smile on my face, extremely happy with the outcome of the date. I almost had half of mind to lean on the door and sigh like the love-sick girls do in the movies.

I didn't. Instead, I took off my boots, throwing them to the side. I smiled wider, thinking about the way Olivia's lips felt on mine. I was so hopeless.

In the living room, I could hear the TV on, so I walked to it. Gwen sat on the couch, with legs propped up on the coffee table watching what looked to be *Keeping Up with the*

Kardashians. She finally tore her eyes away from the screen to look at me.

"What are you smiling about?" Gwen smirked, she clearly knew what I was smiling about. I didn't say anything. Instead, I went over to her and laid down on top of her with my head on her lap and my legs propped up on the armrest.

I don't know why I did it because normally, I'm not that touchy-feely when it comes to people, especially Gwen. But lately, I felt like we were becoming closer which I was immensely happy about.

"What are you doing?" Gwen asked. I could tell she really didn't mind from the slight smile on her face. She seemed more amused than angry.

"Lying down. What does it look like I'm doing?" I said smiling up at her as she looked down at me. "Didn't you want to know what happened on the date?" Usually, I wouldn't be so easy with giving up information, but this time I was dying to just tell somebody.

"I do, but that doesn't mean you can lay your fat ass on me," Gwen said, shoving me in the shoulder, making me titter over the edge a little bit. In retaliation, I began slapping her on the stomach, causing her to laugh.

"Stop it! I thought you were going to tell me about your date, not abuse me."

"I was until you called me fat and tried to push me off," I said with a cheeky grin, enjoying our banter. It wasn't often where I could do this with my sister.

"Just tell me already," Gwen said exasperatedly.

"Fine," I said before telling her the details of the date, with exaggerated hand motions and everything. I skated around the kisses because I really didn't want to share that with Gwen. She seemed happy enough with the things that I did tell her. When I finished telling her, she just stared with amusement in her eyes.

"So, you had fun?"

127

"Loads of it. I had an amazing time," I said with a happy sigh, closing my eyes thinking about Olivia again.

"You really like her?"

"Yes, I do," I said shyly. I felt my phone vibrate in my pocket. Immediately, I knew that it was Olivia. I dug it out quickly.

I had a fantastic time. We should do it again? Goodnight.

I smiled widely, fingers flying over the keyboard rapidly texting her back.

Me too. We should! G' night.

When I finished texting her, Gwen spoke up. "Is that her?" I nodded, still reveling in the fact that Olivia had texted me.

"You should let her know that I'll kill her if she breaks your heart."

~

It has been a week since our first date, and we still haven't gone on another one or at least hung out alone. I knew it was because Olivia was busy, but it still made me a little anxious.

She did make up for it though by constantly texting me, walking me to class most of the time while carrying some of my books. Olivia even abandoned her flock of bitches to come and eat lunch with Neal and me. Gwen had even decided she would join her boyfriend and ate lunch with us too. It was all sort of surreal.

I told Neal everything about what happened, and I sort of regretted it because now he won't stop teasing me. He was sure to have a bruise on his arm from the many times I had punched him.

128

I was standing at my locker, listening to Neal rant about how in calculus one of the school football players is always cheating on him and basically taking all the credit for his work. But as usual, you couldn't tell a school official due to the fact that he would risk getting pummeled, so Neal resulted in ranting to me. That's when someone tapped me on the shoulder.

I turned around with a smile on my face excepting it to be Olivia, but it was not. It was Danika.

She stood in front of me with a smirk on her lips and her hand on her hips. I had no idea what she wanted, but I really didn't want to find out. I stepped away from her, not wanting to be closer to her than I needed to be.

"What do you want?" Neal all but growled from behind me.

Danika scoffed, looking at her nails uninterested. "Nothing that concerns you. So why don't you just leave Joey and me alone to talk."

"Anything you have to say to Joey concerns me. I'm staying." I stayed silent, letting Neal defend me.

"Fine. Be her bodyguard." I flinched when she looked at me, stepping away a little more.

"W-what?"

Danika flicked a strand of dark hair out of her face, still looking at me with her black eyelined eyes. "I..." She started but was interrupted when someone, grabbed her by her shirt, slamming her into the lockers. With her back pressed against the lockers, she stared at her attacker.

I was surprised to see that it was Gwen.

Her face was contorted in anger, and if this was a cartoon, I was sure that steam would be coming out her ears. Gwen was clutching Danika's shirt so hard her knuckles were turning white. Seeing her like this was a little frightening.

I almost stepped forward to get Gwen off her, but Neal put his hand on my shoulder stopping me. He shook his head. Clearly, Neal wanted to know what was going on and I'm pretty

129

sure he wanted to see Gwen beat the shit out of Danika. I had to agree with him.

"What the hell are you doing?" Danika choked out, struggling in Gwen's grip.

"What the fuck did you do to my sister?" Gwen growled through a clenched jaw.

"I don't know what you're talking about?" Danika said, feigning innocence, but Gwen wasn't having it. She slammed Danika into the locker, causing her head to bounce off the lockers.

A crowd was starting to form around us, everyone gaping at the scene. Most, including me, were a little scared for Danika. I scanned the crowd quickly, wondering where Olivia was.

"Nolan told me what you did to Joey!"

"I was going to apologize before you interrupted," Danika sneered, bearing her teeth at Gwen. Again, Gwen really didn't seem to care at this point.

"Like hell you were! You mess with my sister, you mess with me." I was astonished. I have never seen Gwen at like this before. She used to just skate through life without giving me a second glance, not really caring when people at the school bothered me. This was like a completely different Gwen.

Apparently, this was escalating more than everyone thought it would. Gwen looked like she was about to blow. Where were the teachers?

The crowd began to shift as someone made their way through. Someone had finally decided they didn't want to see Danika's blood all over the hall.

Olivia shoved her way through, shooting me a quick glance and going over to Gwen. She put her hand on Gwen's shoulder, trying to console her.

"She's not worth it," Olivia said merely.

Gwen glared one more time then let go. Danika immediately started rubbing the spot were Gwen gripped her shirt, still looking a little shaken. Danika took that as her chance to get the hell out of there before Gwen changed her mind.

"Mess with my sister again, and I'll have your throat!" Gwen shouted after her.

Gwen was about to make her exit when she looked over at me and winked. I grinned at her, letting her know I appreciated it. Gwen smiled back then pushed her way through the dispersing crowd.

"Crazy stuff huh?" Olivia said, sighing glad the crisis was averted.

"Definitely," I said back, still with a huge grin on my face. I used to think that my family really didn't care about me, but Gwen proved me wrong. Well, my parents still didn't, but I was glad she did.

CHAPTER 18
Under the Stars

Sometime during the week, we were finally able to go out on another date. Olivia asked me again this time. I was going to ask her, but it's much harder than it looks. I just couldn't gather up the courage.

Olivia knew I had wanted to be the one to ask but brushed it off, saying it really didn't matter who asked who if we were together. I responded by blushing heavily and stuttering some incoherent answer.

Olivia picked me up at my house again around nine, so it was already dark out. Once again, she didn't tell me where we were going even after I asked multiple times.

I liked surprises, but it was killing me to not know where we were going, especially after we turned off onto a secluded dirt road. Of course, Olivia still didn't answer my questions.

"This area seriously looks like something out of a slasher flick," I said, looking through the windows at the dark, ominous trees. It really did look creepy out there.

Olivia just smiled cryptically and continued concentrating on the road, since it was dark out here.

I decided to not to focus on the drive and stared down at my camera that I had brought along per Olivia's request, deleting the pictures that were useless so I could make more space for photos later.

Finally, the car stopped at what looked like the end of the dirt road. Olivia put the car in park then unlocked our doors. When we got out the car, she went to the trunk, pulling out a blanket and a backpack.

Olivia came over to me, grabbed my hand, moved toward the front of the car and stood at the end of the dirt road.

"All we got to do is walk forward through those trees then there's a grass clearing," she said, not being able to suppress a broad smile.

"Are you serious? You want me to walk in there?" I said indecisively, staring at the dense dark trees in front of us.

"Yes. If you trust me, you will." I knew I would be walking through the dark forest in a few moments because I completely trusted her.

I nodded. "I trust you." Olivia's eyes lit up in the darkness with happiness.

"Good." Olivia took my hand pulling me into the forest. I instantly took to her side, slightly scared of what lurked out there in the woods.

We walked for about a minute or so with me rapidly looking around at each little noise I heard. Olivia just clutched my hand tightly, reassuring me that she would protect me which I was glad for.

We finally broke from the trees and into the clearing. There wasn't much as expected from an abandoned clearing. The grass was about tall enough to go up to about my shin, but I think it was because I was short. There weren't any magnificent blooming flowers all over the place, it was just mostly grass.

But even though the area was pretty plain, it was filled with various noises; crickets and cicadas were chirping from their hiding places, and you could faintly hear an owl hooting from the trees. The stars shined brightly above us, along with the moon lighting the way for Olivia to find a comfortable spot for us to sit.

When she did, Olivia laid out the blanket she had been carrying on to the ground. She sat, pulling me down close to her, both of us sitting Indian style.

Before Olivia unzipped the backpack she had brought, she said, "Okay, so I didn't have one of those wicker picnic baskets people always seem to have in movies, so I just put the food in this backpack." I nodded, letting her continue. I didn't really care what she carried the food in, but she looked cute trying to explain it to me.

"Okay, so I know that one time you told me that you don't like sandwiches that have been put in a sandwich bag, so I didn't bring any." I smiled knowing she remembered that about me and it was adorable how she seemed to be rambling at this point.

As Olivia began pulling things out her bag, she named them off. "I brought bananas, apples, strawberries, pineapples, pretzels, and last but not least to go with of this Nutella. I also brought apple juice, figuring you would want to stay away from alcohol for a while."

"Awesome," I said in approval because I loved Nutella, and Olivia brought all the right stuff to dip in it. I really did find it a good idea to stay away from alcohol, considering the last time I had it.

"I'm glad you liked it. I didn't really know if you would," Olivia said nervously, wringing her hands. I grabbed one, making her stop and look at me.

"It's perfect. All of it," I spoke sincerely.

"So, do I get to feed you this time without you resisting?"

I groaned but nodded, seeing the pout Olivia had on her lips. For some reason, my confidence rose when I was around Olivia because I leaned forward, giving her a peck on the lips. I smiled when I pulled away, seeing the surprised look on her face.

I did let her feed me like I had agreed. We finished off the entire Nutella using the food she had brought along as scoops, and sometimes, we just licked it off a spoon. It was appealing either way. I took plenty of pictures of us together; some with just Olivia eating Nutella and smiling. I also took a couple when we decided it was a good idea to put the Nutella on our faces.

When we were satisfied, we laid down on the blanket, staring up at the stars. Our hands were in a comfortable position between the two of us. It was all very surreal once again, being here with Olivia.

"I would take this time to be romantic and point at the stars and tell you all about them, but I don't know jack shit, so instead, I will use my imagination," Olivia said with a broad smile. I laughed a little at her being silly.

"Sounds good to me."

"Okay, well that one there," Olivia started pointing to a bright and big compared to the other stars. "That star is well known by everybody because it's beautiful, you see. Everyone is always surrounding it, trying to be in the light that it shares."

"But the star, as it turns out, was never happy because it was different from every other star and the other stars always seem to want something from it." I examined Olivia's face as she stared up at the stars. It no longer seemed like this was just a story about some star.

She continued with a sort of faraway look in her eyes. "One day, the star mistakenly found the most beautiful thing it had ever seen. It was clearly different from everyone else, so the star was immediately taken with her." Olivia didn't even notice her slip up by saying 'her' rather than talking about the stars.

Olivia stopped staring at the stars and looked at me. Her eyes flickered back and forth, searching mine. "The star's life has never been the same since." She finished in a whisper.

I didn't know what to say after that. I was hopeless compared to her heated stare. Everything she wanted to say,

Olivia was clearly saying it through her eyes. Emotions were swirling all around, but I still understood what she was trying to tell me.

I felt the same way about her. Ever since she had kissed me the first time, my entire life was put at a tilt. At first, I thought it was a bad thing, involving myself with her. But I realized now that Olivia was definitely the greatest thing to ever happen to me.

"I'm pretty sure she feels the same way," I said finally, grinning at her. Olivia grinned back, scooting closer to me and briefly brushing her lips against mine. Olivia didn't let it go farther than that because she seemed to have more to say.

Olivia sat up and hugged her knees to her chest, looking up at the sky. I followed suit sitting up Indian style, waiting for her to speak.

"I was going to ask you this when we were on the Ferris wheel at the carnival, but I thought it was way too cliché," Olivia said with a small smile.

"This is just as clichéd as the Ferris wheel."

"Shut up, you're ruining the moment," Olivia snapped playfully while giggling. "I didn't ask you also because I was way too nervous. It was like every time I wanted to, it just got stuck in my throat." I knew whatever she had to tell me was hard because she admitted being nervous about it, and I absolutely knew the feeling.

"You can ask me now." I urged, trying to help. Apparently, it worked because Olivia turned on me with determination evident in her eyes and features; there was also a sparkle of hope.

"Will you be my girlfriend?"

My face blushed crimson red in the darkness. This was the first time anyone has ever asked me that, so imagine my surprise. Everything I was thinking and feeling were all moving so fast that I couldn't process them. I ducked my head for a moment, still trying to gather my thoughts.

136

"Okay, you don't have to say anything. I completely understand. I pushed you too quickly. I don't even know why after a month or so, you would even consider going out with me," Olivia rambled quickly. Before she could take another breathe so that she could ramble some more, I reached up and gently grabbed the sides of her face.

It must have done something because Olivia stopped talking right away. I smiled at her, trying to ease her fast-track mind.

"Yes, I will," I answered softly. Olivia breathed a heavy sigh of relief at hearing my voice. I let go of her face, smiling giddily at Olivia. "What made you think I would say no?"

Olivia just giggled and shrugged. "I don't know. You just didn't respond at first, so I thought the worst." I laughed along with her not being able to help myself.

After our laughs quieted down, Olivia said, "You really want to be my girlfriend?" I grinned scooting close to her again, putting my arm around her waist and laying my head on her shoulder. Olivia responded by putting her arm around my shoulder, pulling me closer. I couldn't believe that I was pressed so close to her and the fact that I was now her girlfriend.

"More than anything."

CHAPTER 19
Perfect

Things were going great so far between Olivia and me, now that we were officially together and I was her girlfriend. I would never get tired of saying that. It just seemed too natural.

We still hadn't decided how to go about being a couple in school. It was awkward not knowing if I could hold her hand on the way to class or was I allowed to just hug her out of the blue. Luckily, we didn't hang out much during school, so I didn't have to ponder these urges for long.

What we did decide though was that I wasn't ready to tell my parents about my relationship with Olivia. Olivia's parents already knew, since they didn't have a problem with Olivia dating girls. They promised to keep it between themselves until we were ready for that kind of exposure.

It was more like when I was ready for that kind of exposure. Olivia was fine with being who she was and dating me (which still seems unreal), but I was still trying to process everything in a sense.

I didn't know how my parents would take it. I was sure that my dad would not care, since he mostly only cared about his job. It was just my mother's opinion that I was afraid of. I knew she would approve of the whole me spending more time with Olivia, only because it improved her image. But if I told her that we were together, that's just a whole different story.

In her eyes, her image would be tarnished. To her, her already defective daughter was still bound to have the perfect life she was having. By perfect life, I mean one with a nice house, a lump sum of money, and let's not forget the small detail of having a husband. Oh, and think of the gossip at the country club when they found out her daughter actually wanted a wife instead of a husband. My mother wouldn't be able to deal with it.

I don't know what it was about me that my mother didn't like. Maybe it was the fact that I tried to think for myself and rather not look like a bimbo.

I didn't want to think of that though. Instead, I opted to think about how Olivia would be here in a few minutes so that we could have sort of a movie night. Being home alone most of the time was great for times like these.

I was jumping out of my skin with excitement. I was always excited to see Olivia. I had already set out tons of coma-inducing goodies and picked out a few movies for us to choose from.

The doorbell rang, announcing Olivia's arrival. I bounded over to the door, swinging it open with a large grin on my face.

Olivia looked equally as happy, smiling with a box of pizza.

"Hi," I said taking the box from her hands and opening it to look at its contents. Pineapple and ham pizza. My favorite.

I inhaled the mouth water aroma before saying, "You sure do know how to please a girl."

Olivia shrugged nonchalantly while shutting the door. "I try," she quipped then leaned over and kissed me on the cheek. My face warmed considerably from the simple contact.

"Already picked out a couple of movies but you can pick which one you want," I said carrying the box of pizza into the living room, setting it down on the coffee table next to all the other goodies.

"Before we watch the movie, I was thinking we could post the pictures we took on your wall," Olivia said with a sort of shy smile. "I mean if you want. We don't have to."

139

"I'd love to." I began to head upstairs with Olivia following behind me. I could tell she was staring at me, but I didn't mind since I was her girlfriend now. I still wasn't used to that.

When we made it to my room, I went over to my desk and opened the drawer that held the photos and Olivia's jacket. I had forgotten all about it, I pulled it out along with the photos.

"Wow, I forgot I had given that to you," Olivia said over my shoulder.

"You can have it back," I said, extending the jacket to her. Olivia looked thoughtful for a moment before she spoke.

"You keep it."

"Really?"

"Yeah. It looks better on you." Her comment made a smile appear on my face. Of course, I wasn't going to refuse keeping something of hers.

"Let's find a place to put these," I said waving the pictures around.

We found the perfect place near my bed. The bulletin board was pretty crowded, so I removed all the pictures and put them away leaving the whole area just for us. Olivia immediately started sticking photographs on it. I just watched, leaving her to it.

"Done," she proclaimed. I hadn't realized how many pictures we had taken until they were all posted.

"It looks good." It really did. It made my stomach do little flips, seeing all of the photos of us together on my wall. We looked happy and carefree. My favorite had to be the one with us sporting huge grins and Nutella smeared all over our faces.

"One last thing," Olivia said before going over to the board and taking at least three photos down. "I want to keep these. I don't have any pictures of you." I blushed at the prospect of Olivia having pictures of me in her room.

"Now, how about that movie?" Olivia said with a smirk and a mischievous glint in her brown eyes.

140

"O-okay." I squeaked out. I didn't know why I was nervous all of a sudden, but I think it was because the way Olivia was looking at me just now.

As we walked out of my room, I heard a door slam. I flinched when I saw a perfectly styled blonde hair from over the banister. My mother was home for some reason. I made my way down the stairs, with my head bowed.

"Josephine!" She shrieked upon seeing the living room. "What is all this mess? What have I told you about eating so much? You're already not that pretty, no need to get fat too." I flinched again at my mother's words; she didn't even let me explain.

It looked like she was about to yell again when she saw Olivia standing behind me. My mother immediately straightened up and put a large, but fake, smile on her face. "Olivia, I didn't see you there. It's nice to have you over."

Before she responded, Olivia looked at me with concern. But I didn't meet her eyes, I stared at the floor instead. "Thanks for having me."

"Josephine, you didn't ask if you could have guest over." My mother said with a cold smile.

"I-I didn't know that I h-had to." Which was true since I didn't have friends over often. Neal and I usually spent our time at his house because mine always felt so cold and empty compared to his.

"Next time, make sure that you do. I'm only here to freshen up so carry on." She glared at me for a moment, clearly angry that someone in her circle saw her true colors. "Have a nice time." My mother said only to Olivia.

"Will do, Mrs. Montgomery."

A lump began to form in my throat as I watched my mother go upstairs. It slowly began to fade when Olivia laced her fingers through mine. I really wish Olivia hadn't been around for that, but from the look in her eyes, I could tell she didn't care about my mother. She was only concerned with me.

Olivia, not saying anything, pulled me into the living room and over to the couch. We plopped down right next to each other. We didn't say anything until we heard my mother say a distant goodbye and the front door slam.

Olivia was the one that broke the silence that had settled between us. "Why does your mother act like that toward you?" Olivia said with a questioning gaze.

I looked away from her and looked at my hands in my lap. "So you have noticed," I said with a bitter chuckle.

"It's hard to miss when she talks to you like that or doesn't at all." Olivia voiced softly, grabbing my hand pulling it to her lap.

"It's because I'm not Gwen." Olivia just looked at me, waiting for me to elaborate. I was hoping she would just leave it at that, but I guess not.

"Gwen is the daughter that she had always wanted and I'm just not. If you haven't noticed, I get nervous when I'm around people I don't know well and start to stutter. I don't dress glamorously because those clothes make me feel uncomfortable." I took a breath not wanting to continue, but it all came spilling out anyways. "I don't get the best grades, and I have no aspirations that my mother approves of. So in her eyes, I'm just a failure." I finished dejectedly, blinking rapidly trying to chase away the prickling behind my eyes.

Olivia put her hand under my chin, pulling my face up to look at hers. Olivia's brown eyes stared at me so intensely, searching my eyes for a moment before her features softened.

"In my eyes, you're perfect." I really didn't know what to say after that. Butterflies were raging in my stomach and Olivia's scent wrapped around me, comforting me. I really didn't care anymore about my mother or what she had said. Now, I only cared about the girl hovering so close to me.

Olivia clearly felt the shift in mood because her body relaxed into mine and she moved her lips much closer to mine. This time, Olivia didn't wait for me to make the first move.

Olivia leaned in and smoothly captured my lips in hers. The contact instantly sent electricity through my body, sparking all the way down to my fingertips and toes.

I couldn't help but relax my body against hers, pulling my arms up to rest around her neck. Olivia took them as a sign to press forward, moving my body until my back is against the armrest. I was pretty sure that my heart was about to combust at how rapidly it was beating in my chest.

Somewhere in between us kissing, one of my legs had elevated itself, lying flat on the couch causing Olivia to darn near straddle my waist. Olivia's tongue glided over my lips causing me to gasp, giving her complete access which she took immediately.

I really didn't know how a confession of my sad life turned into a make-out session, but I had to say that I was not complaining.

I was certain that if the world ended around us, I would not notice nor care.

Sadly, what I did notice was the front door slamming. Usually, your first reaction would have been to break apart, but no. My first reaction was to push Olivia off me. My reaction caused her to land on the floor noisily.

Gwen and Neal walked into the living room, hearing the noise, hand in hand. Olivia was still on the floor, rubbing her backside. Olivia's face was flushed red, and I was pretty sure my face looked exactly the same.

Gwen and Neal looked at each other with identical smirks, obviously piecing together what was going on. "Are we interrupting something?"

"No," I said just as Olivia said, "Yes." I whipped around to gawk at Olivia. She just shrugged, picking herself up off the floor then sat down next to me.

"What? They are being total cockblocks!" Olivia said exasperatedly, sitting next to me with an adorable frown that just made me want to kiss all her frown lines.

"But they didn't have to know that."

"They already do! Just look at their smug little faces." It was true. They did look smug staring at us. "Why are you guys even here?"

"Gwen heard Joey on the phone talking about your movie night, so we decided to crash it," Neal said shrugging. "Hope you don't mind," Neal said innocently, acting like he didn't know what he was doing.

Neal walked over to sit on the other couch having to cross over Olivia's legs, which was a bad move because she took the opportunity to trip him. "Of course not," Olivia said sarcastically as Neal stumbled a little before sitting.

Somewhere between my whirlwind of a relationship with Olivia, Neal and Olivia actually started to become good friends, which I was pleased about. Gwen didn't seem to mind Olivia much either.

"Great!" Gwen added walking over to sit next to Neal. "Now, what are we watching?"

"Clearly nothing," Neal mumbled, but everyone heard him. Gwen elbowed him in the side causing him to let a loud yelp to escape.

"How about *X-men First Class*?" I said in an effort to cover the clear awkwardness. I got up hastily, popping in the DVD and grabbing a bowl of popcorn and two slices of pizza for Olivia and me from the coffee table. I reached behind me, dimming the lights, trying not to give Neal a chance to say anything more.

As the movie began to play, Olivia put her arm around my shoulder, pulling me closer. I looked at her face then watching as the movie lights played over her creamy skin.

Looking at Olivia's soft plump lips in the dim light, I realized how much I agreed with her. Gwen and Neal were such cockblocks.

CHAPTER 20
Awkward Diner Moments

I clicked open my locker slowly, already exhausted, and it was only third period. I shoved my books roughly in it, not caring the order that it was in.

My locker was even more crowded with photos than it was before. Olivia insisted on putting pictures of her along with the others, and since it's a well-known fact that girls love taking selfies of themselves, there were quite a few.

I didn't really mind, I guess it came with the whole relationship thing, or maybe it was just an Olivia thing. I wasn't really a relationship expert since this was my first real relationship with someone. It was kind of scary not knowing what the do's and don'ts of relationships were.

I always wondered, in the back of my mind, what if I did something to mess our relationship? Or even worse, what if Olivia realized I wasn't what she wanted? I was obviously way out of her league, which was an untouchable goddess.

I shook my head, not wanting to think about that being a possibility.

I slammed my locker shut a little harder than I should have. Olivia stood on the other side of it, staring at me with a pout. She looked absolutely adorable with her lip poked out in such a way. I just want to kiss her, but again, I didn't know if I was allowed to in a crowded hallway full of people. There really should be a handbook for this kind of stuff.

"What's with the pout?" I said with a slightly mocking tone, smiling a little bit.

"We can't go that diner you like so much after school."
I began pouting too. Olivia had taken me out one night to this
amazing diner. It had a cool authentic atmosphere with an old
jukebox, checked tiles, and a greasy old cook and everything.
And it didn't hurt that the milkshakes were awesome. I always
had a craving for them.

Olivia and I had planned to go buy some today after
school, but apparently, we couldn't do that now.

"Aww, why?" I whined. I was really looking forward to
having a milkshake and spending time with Olivia after a long
day at school.

"Student council announced that there was going to be
an emergency after school meeting and I have to go since I am
the student body president," Olivia said with slumped shoulders
and a pout, still protruding from her mouth.

I sighed heavily, making a pout identical to hers. "We
can always go some other time."

"I know, but I wanted to go with you today," Olivia
said. But before I could respond, someone spoke up beside me.

"Joey, can I talk to you?" The voice said. I turned away
from Olivia when I heard the voice and immediately stepped
back when I noticed who the speaker was.

Danika stood before me with a blank look on her face
and arms crossed over her chest. Olivia seeing Danika
immediately stepped in front of me with a dark look.

"What do you want Danika?" Olivia growled.

Danika's blank face immediately morphed into her
signature smirk. "You sure have a lot of bodyguards, Joey. Are
there any more I should know about?"

"Do I need to repeat myself?" Olivia asked. I noticed
that her anger mounting as her fist clenched at her sides.

"Fine, I just wanted to talk to Joey," Danika said, finally
giving up on her smart-ass comments. Olivia crossed her arms
over her chest defensively, not trusting Danika's motive. I don't
think I really trusted her either.

146

"Really, I just wanted to apologize. Last time I tried, I was attacked, and now you're shielding her like she is fine china that needs to be protected."

Olivia looked at Danika with apprehension, still not saying anything for a moment, mulling over Danika's words. "I'll leave, but I won't be far," Olivia said before leaning over and kissing me on the cheek, showing off her possessiveness. I didn't mind. I actually thought her trying to protect me was kind of cute.

Danika cringed a little at the show of affection, watching as Olivia walked down the hall away from us.

Danika stood there, not speaking at first, just staring. "I'm sorry for having Nolan spike your drink then forcing myself on you. It was a fucked up thing for me to do. Can you forgive me?"

I didn't say anything. I looked at her, trying to see if she really meant it or had ulterior motives. I couldn't find anything hiding behind her dark eyes.

"N-no, I don't forgive you. Do you think you can j-just say sorry like it didn't happen?" I whispered, still not feeling overly comfortable in Danika's presence.

Danika looked dejected, but I just couldn't bring myself to care much, not after what she had done. "Okay..." She lingered for just a moment, examining me. "I'll see you around."

Olivia appeared at my side as soon as Danika had sauntered away around the corner. "I don't trust her. You shouldn't either." I was going to respond, but the class bell interrupted me.

"I don't. Let's get to class," I said instead. Olivia nodded in agreement, and then she took my hand, pulling me in the direction of our classes.

I don't know why but whenever Olivia and Danika interacted, I felt like there was more bad blood between them than just what happened at the part. For now, I would just shrug it off.

147

~

School was finally over, and I was dragging my body out the door of that hellhole and toward my car in the school parking lot.

I skillfully navigated my way around the big meat-headed lacrosse players and their high-pitched girlfriends that were near my car.

I tried to ignore them the best I could as I clicked the unlock button on my car keys. Just as I was opening the door and getting in, I noticed something out of the corner of my eye.

My front tire was flat. I sighed loudly in heavy frustration, slamming the door back shut and stomped over to the tire. It was so deflated I knew I wouldn't be able to get home.

I crouched next to it, inspecting it for the damage. I couldn't see any evident damage, so I just guessed the inner tube had popped. I growled at the inanimate object like it would help the situation when it clearly wouldn't.

I leaned against the car in defeat, pulling out my phone to text Neal.

Where are you? My car has a flat. I need a ride home.

I only had to wait a few moments before he responded.

On the football field, waiting for Gwen to finish practice. We were getting something to eat afterward. You're welcome to join.

I grimaced to myself. I really didn't want to be the third wheel, having to sit quietly while they flirted shamelessly with each other.

—I think I'll pass but thanks. I'll just walk home.
—Okay, be safe.

148

I put my phone away and started making my way out of the parking lot. I would probably have to call a tow truck to come and take it to the repair shop. That would probably drain most of my savings I had put up for a rainy day. Today, it seemed to be raining like a bitch.

I trudged down the street, still not anywhere near my house. The sidewalk just seemed to be getting longer and longer, mocking me. Usually, I liked to walk but today just wasn't one of those days.

I began kicking a pebble as I walked, trying to pass the time.

I suddenly heard a rumble of a car engine as it passed by. I didn't look up since I didn't care to see who it was.

I did look up when I noticed the car backtrack and pull up beside me. I kept walking, not in favor of being attacked by a predator.

"Joey!" The driver called out my name. I turned, really not expecting to see Danika in the driver's seat.

I groaned, really not wanting to deal with her at this point. "W-what?"

"Where you going?" Danika asked nonchalantly as if she was trying to start an actual conversation with me.

"Home." I would have said something in the smart ass category, but I just wasn't feeling it.

"Let me take you." My jaw almost dropped. She really didn't just ask me to get in the car with her. She clearly could see my apprehension because she said, "It's about to rain. If you don't get in now, you will look like a drowned rat before you can even get home."

I titled my head to the sky. Of course, she was right. I hadn't even noticed the dark, ominous clouds before.

I groaned out loud, not really wanting to get into her car (especially not with her), but I knew that I had to, unless I wanted to be soaking wet. I stomped over to the passenger's side door, threw it open, and got into her cherry red 2017 Ford Mustang. I took a moment to marvel at the interior before roughly putting on my seatbelt and slumping in my seat.

Danika just smiled a wide victorious smile before putting the car into drive again.

"T-this doesn't mean I trust you. Let alone like you." Danika smiled anyway, "Duly noted."

"Go straight till you get to Avon then make a right then another right on the second street," I instructed, wanting her to take me home as soon as possible. As I said that, I could see rain droplets fall against the window pane. I didn't want to admit that Danika had been right.

"No problem." We sat in silence after that. She probably didn't know what to say to me, and I just didn't want to talk to her.

I looked out the window, trying to distract myself from the awkward suffocating silence. I began to notice that the street we were driving on was not the way to my house.

"W-where are we going?" I said nervously. I knew I shouldn't have gotten in the car with her.

"Just to get something to eat. I thought I should treat you to something as a better apology than I gave you earlier."

"I don't want a-anything to eat. I-I want to go home." I probably sounded like a whiny baby right now, but I really did just want to go home, and I didn't want to have to deal with her any longer than I needed too.

"Sure," Danika said. "After we get something to eat." I groaned loudly slammed my head against the cool window. Apparently, there was no changing her mind.

We soon pulled into the parking lot of the last place I wanted to eat at with Danika. Coincidently, we pulled into the exact place that Olivia and I had been planning to eat at.

"D-do we have to eat here?" I said with a small voice.

"Yes, this place is awesome," Danika said, quickly scrambling out of the car and running to the door to get out of the rain.

I sighed, getting out of the car at a slower pace than she did, not really minding the rain.

Danika held open the door for me as we walked into the diner. The familiar smell of unhealthy delicious food immediately made me feel guilty for being here with Danika and not Olivia.

Danika slid into a booth nearest to us, and I followed suit. It didn't take long for a waiter to walk up to take our orders.

"I'll just have a hamburger and fries," Danika said the waiter, who nodded and scribbled it down on his notepad.

"A milkshake for me." It was all I wanted; I wasn't starving anymore. The waiter walked away swiftly to go put in our orders.

"So…" Danika trailed out. "Are you and Olivia like an item now?"

I thought for a moment before answering. I didn't know if I wanted to tell other people still, especially Danika, about us. I didn't want it traveling through the grapevine and getting back to my mother. But Danika didn't really seem like the gossiping type. Also, Olivia kissing me on the cheek in front of her kind of already confirmed it. So I nodded.

"Oh," Danika said solemnly.

Silence then fell over our table; only the sounds of plates clattering in the kitchen and the conversation of others filled the silence.

"Truth is," Danika spoke up, "I brought you here because I don't want you to think I'm a complete conniving she-bitch that I seem to be." I snorted at her comment, not believing her for a second. Danika's face scrunched up with anger at the noise.

"Look, I'm trying to be your friend here," she snapped.

151

"L-like I want to be your friend after you drugged and sexually harassed me."

For an odd reason, Danika cracked a smile. "I did do that, didn't I? It was really a shitty thing to do, I know that. How about we start over?"

I contemplated it for a moment. I didn't really like having all this pent up anger storing inside me, but I also didn't want to trust her so easily either.

I couldn't bring myself to agree nor disagree. My words lodged in my throat, and I knew that if I tried to say anything, my words would trip over one another.

Danika smiled happily then stuck her hand out towards me as if to shake my own. When I placed my hand in hers, she said, "Danika Vasquez, nice to meet you."

I couldn't help but smile just a little bit. "Josephine Montgomery, but you can call me Joey." We shook each other's hands firmly.

Our food arrived shortly after. I still felt really bad about being here without Olivia, but I couldn't help but relish the cold dessert as it spread over my body.

As we sat their together, I realized that I had never asked why Danika dare do what she had done. Based on the terms that we were on, I wasn't sure that I could. I knew that this could all just blow up in my face. Time will only tell.

CHAPTER 21
Optimism and Puzzle Pieces

Soon after Danika dropped me off at my house, I went upstairs to take a shower. Half because the muggy feeling of rain made me feel dirty and also because I needed to think about Danika of course.

Sure, I shook hands with her in a sort of truce, but that didn't mean I trusted her. Every time Olivia was around when Danika was near, I always felt like something was off. I just couldn't put my finger on it. I just didn't trust her.

I was tired of being mad with Danika. I wasn't used to being angry for such a long time, but that was mostly because I didn't have many friends to be mad at. When I was mad at Neal, it was usually over something dumb, so there was no use in holding a grudge. Grudges aren't my thing. But I guess what Danika had done called for much more than a grudge. Maybe a black eye instead.

I finished my shower, stepping out of the bathroom with a t-shirt and some basketball shorts. My hair was still damp with some drops of water dripping down onto the back of my shirt.

Gwen was sitting criss-crossed on my bed, reading a magazine which I'm sure she could have been doing in her room, but I was actually glad she was here. Ever since she and I have gotten closer, I don't really like being in an empty house as much as I used to.

"Let me braid your hair, I want to try this new braid called the waterfall braid." I shrugged, not really caring. I loved the feeling of someone playing in my hair, so I didn't mind.

I sat on the floor, leaning on the bed letting Gwen scoot up behind me, draping her legs on the side of me. She started working immediately, running her fingers through my light hair. I pulled my glasses off, setting them on the side of me, closing my eyes and relaxing into her touch.

"Soooo, you and Olivia are together right?" Gwen said, breaking the silence. I had forgotten all about telling her. With her and Neal walking in on us making out, I just thought it was safe to assume that we were together officially.

"Yes," I said, not even blinking an eye about telling Gwen.

"Good for you. I'm glad you have found someone you actually like. I also thought it was strange that you two were going at it and you weren't together." My face flushed red at her comment. I really wished she would just forget about it.

"What did mom say about it?" I scoffed at her question.

"Like I told mom. She would die then come back to life so she could tell me how much of an embarrassment I am. No, thank you." I really believed me being in a relationship with Olivia would not go over well with my mother. I was surprised that she hasn't been told about us yet. But then again, Olivia and I weren't the type to show much PDA in school, so it was unlikely a lot of people picked up on us being together.

"I don't think it would be that bad. She might even be happy that you're socializing and your girlfriend is both popular with the parents and teenagers."

"I highly doubt that."

"You never know, she might."

I laughed out loud this time at her optimism.

~

Lunch was sort of a relaxing affair now that I was able to sit with not only just Neal but Olivia too. Classes went by in a flash, but I think that was mostly because I fell asleep through half of them. Gwen and I decided after she finished braiding my hair, to stay up later than usual, watching movies and pigging out.

Neal sat in front of me with his books and papers laid out in front of him, studying for a test we were to have a week from now. Obviously, he wasn't normal because people like me would wait until the day before to start studying. It was a strategic way to keep all the information fresh in your head. Who am I kidding? It was just my way of procrastination.

I watched him as he skimmed the pages quickly, stopping only a couple of times to write notes. My lunch was just a small bag of chips and a Capri Sun. I wasn't really a lunch eating type of person, so this was enough for me.

But I was bored out of my mind, just sitting here, watching Neal's eyes look over the rim of his glasses at his books.

Thankfully, Olivia came out of nowhere and kissed me on the cheek quickly before sitting down next to me, bumping my shoulders slightly. Neal only lifted his head for a moment, giving Olivia a small nod of acknowledgment then went back to studying.

"What's up?" she said, peeling back the banana she had in her hand and taking a bite.

"Not much. I was just about to gouge my eyes in boredom. You almost missed it, you came just in time."

"Good thing too," Olivia smirked, propping her elbow up on the table staring at me and continued to stare as I ate my food. She held an apple in her hand which she quickly finished off then tossed it into the trash near us. "So what did you do after I bailed on you?"

Of course, she would bring it up. I was hoping I wouldn't have to tell her about my activities yesterday. But now that she asked, I didn't want to lie, so I had to tell her. I knew she wouldn't like it, not that I was too fond of Danika either. It

155

just she seemed to not like Danika at all, even before she drugged me. I didn't want to unleash that fury.

"I kind of had a milkshake without you," I said hanging my head in shame, not looking her in the eye.

"Aww really?" Olivia said with a playful sort of pout.

"Yeah, but that's not even the worst part. It's the person that I was with that is the kicker." Olivia's face then got serious as she tried to catch my eye.

"Who were you with?"

"Danika." Olivia visibly flinched, scooting an inch or two away from me, looking me directly in the face looking for something in my eyes.

"If you're trying to be funny, it's not working."

"I'm serious. I was w-with Danika." I even had the face to match the tone of my voice.

"Why in the hell where you with Danika?" Olivia said with an edge to her voice. It was my turn to flinch this time.

"L-long story short, flat tire plus rain equals Danika d-driving me home, which really meant her driving me to the diner," I said all in a rush, trying to get it out in one breathe.

"You didn't have to go with her."

"I-I wasn't planning on getting milkshakes with her, it just so happened that she wouldn't let me go home and insisted we eat something. And she chose the diner."

"Last time she forced you into something it didn't turn out so good. You shouldn't trust her." There's that feeling I keep having about something else going on between them. The way she said those words made it seem like there was some underlying scar that I didn't know about.

"I'm not. It's just that she apologized, and I'm tired of being angry all the time. I'm just over it," I said, shrugging in indifference. I don't think I'd really ever be over it, but it was just my personality to move forward instead of dwelling. I wanted to focus on the good. Then I started to smile brightly,

156

"And one good thing did come out of her forcing herself on to me."

"What's that?"

"I probably wouldn't have kissed you, and you wouldn't have asked me out."

"Don't make light of someone forcing themselves on you. But I probably would have still asked you out though" Olivia said with a cocky smirk, leaning forward to kiss me on the cheek again. But was interrupted when Neal spoke. I had actually almost forgotten he was there.

"Guys, I'm still here," Neal groaned, bringing himself from his studies. "I know you two are still in the honeymoon phase, but Jesus, tone it down a bit when I'm present." I stuck my tongue out at him. He couldn't talk because he and Gwen acted the same way, maybe even worst.

"Whatever," I said, drinking my Capri Sun.

"Joey, we almost just had our first fight," Olivia said with a playful pouty look on her face again. I really did just want to kiss her lips at that moment.

"Luckily, I helped avoid it with my suave flirting," I said, winking at Olivia jokingly. Olivia didn't respond; she just nudged my shoulder while blushing. This new confidence thing around Olivia was really working in my favor.

Someone plopped heavily down on the other side of Olivia, leaning forward so they could look at me. "We should really go back to that diner again don't you think?" Danika said. Speak of the devil. Just as we almost avoid arguing about Danika, she appeared.

I gulped down the lump that had formed in my throat as soon as Danika sat down. Olivia didn't look happy. Neal looked up at the disturbance, his face going blank when he noticed it was Danika. He looked at me inquisitively; I just shrugged, not knowing what to do.

"What, Danika?" Olivia said, with an annoyed sigh. Danika just grinned, looking at me.

"I can't sit with my new friend?" Olivia and Neal looked around, trying to see who she could possibly be talking about. They were oblivious to the fact that she was talking about me. Danika sighed giving up on them, getting the hint. "Joey and I are friends."

Olivia whipped her head towards me. "I told you not to trust her!"

"I-I don't!" I said, trying defending myself. Olivia just searched my face, trying to see if I was lying. She must have believed me because she whipped back around towards Danika.

"A month ago, you didn't want anything to do with me, and now you're trying to make friends with my girlfriend!" Olivia said a little too loud. A couple of people turned to look but then went back to what they were doing moments later.

A hurt look crossed Danika face quickly, but she covered it up with a smirk. "I still don't want anything to with you; I just want your girlfriend."

Olivia snorted then mumbled, "Now you want to be with girls." I think it was not meant to be heard, but I heard it anyways and clearly, so did Neal because he snapped his eyes up to me. My eyes snapped to Olivia. What did that mean?

Olivia flushed red with everyone staring at her now. She stood up abruptly, causing her chair to scrap against the floor. "I'm going to go." Her eyes were steely, and her face was flushed as she leaned down to kiss me on the cheek. She tossed a tiny wave toward Neal and a hard glance at Danika then she stalked away out the cafeteria.

I wanted to run after her, but my legs were frozen in the place. The whole table seemed to freeze in its place. It all happened so fast. One minute Olivia was calm, and the next, smoke was blowing from out her ears. No one was expecting whatever that was that just happened.

But from the look on Danika's face, I think she knew that might happen. I would even say she looked a little crestfallen from Olivia's outburst.

158

I was positive something had happened between Olivia and Danika. If my suspicions were not confirmed from that display, then I don't know what would. Now, all I had to do was find out what that was. But first, I would have to make sure Olivia was okay.

I looked at Neal. He nodded, obviously understanding my inner struggle. I didn't even spare a glance at Danika before I got up and sprinted after Olivia.

CHAPTER 22
Bleacher Confessions

When I ran out of the cafeteria, I didn't see Olivia anywhere. So I began my search by her locker, then the girls' locker room, the auditorium, so on and so forth. I still wasn't able to find her at any of these places.

I decided to check the hill. I looked at all the stone tables trying to see if I could pick out her chocolate brown locks in the crowd of people. I was about to give up when I decided to check one more place.

I jogged toward the football fields, searching for her there. There were guys on the field using their lunch break to toss the football back and forth. I turned my head up toward the bleachers, and that is where Olivia sat with her legs pulled up to her chest and her face was pointed at the sky.

I jogged up the stairs and then sat gently down next to her. After a moment or so, with her still not looking my way, I wrapped my arm around her back and hugged her fiercely.

It was minutes before she actually reacted to the contact. She leaned her head into my chest, staring at me. I noticed that her eyes were a little red stained as if she had been crying.

My heart clutched at the sight. This Danika thing really must have hurt her if she had been crying about it. I didn't want Olivia to cry.

"Tell me what's wrong," I said softly, trying to coax her into telling me what was up with her and Danika.

"You know I don't trust Danika." Yes, I knew she didn't, but there had to be more to it if she had been crying about it.

"Yes, I know. But why?"

Olivia looked at me, looking back and forth at my eyes. I stared back, not knowing what I should do. Olivia sat up, wiping her eyes and running her hands through her hair.

"I'll have to start from the beginning if you want to know the whole story," Olivia said with a reluctant sigh.

"I got time," I said. We really didn't have that much time since class was about to start up again, but I figured the story wouldn't take that long.

"Okay. I'll give you the story of the infamous Danika and me," Olivia said with a sad chuckle. "Once upon a time, when I had just started high school, I was just about as shy as you are." I gave her a look, not believing that the most popular girl and student body president could have ever been shy.

"I know I don't look like it, but I was. I was just used to not speaking for myself, letting my parents and status speak for me, so I was shy when it came to interacting with people."

"So that explains the picture I took of you all by yourself at lunch."

"Yep, I had no friends to speak of back then. But Danika apparently saw something in me because she made it her personal mission to become my friend. I didn't turn her down because like I said, I had no friends. We became best friends, and I started to rise on the social latter once everyone knew I was friends with Danika." Olivia's shoulders slumped a little bit as she told her story. I could say I was not about to like what she was about to tell me next.

"Now, I have to backtrack a little bit." She looked at me from the corner of her eye to see if I was still listening, which I was. "Freshmen year was the year that I realized that I was gay. Apparently, the transition from middle school to high school transformed girls into these..." Olivia had a blush on her cheeks

161

as she spoke. She threw her arms up in frustration, not being able to find the right words. "I don't know; I just know that I thought every girl I laid eyes on was hot."

I smiled a little bit, at the way her younger self thought. She nudged me in the shoulder, not taking to my amusement. "Don't laugh! I was young."

"Fine, fine. Continue."

Olivia put her hand on her chin. "Hmm, where was I?" she said, pretending to lose her spot. "Ah, I know my perversion. I was confused, and then I had Danika as a best friend who just made me more confused. You know how Danika is." I nodded, knowing exactly what she meant since I had firsthand experience with Danika.

"I realized that I had liked Danika, way more than just as a friend." I cringed at her words, not liking the prospect of Olivia liking Danika. It made my stomach sink. Olivia rubbed my arm a little bit trying to reassure me.

"Past tense," Olivia added before continuing. "Being around her made me want to explode, so I finally told her that I was in love with her." This really hurt me. I didn't like the idea of Olivia liking someone else, and I didn't like her loving someone else.

"I don't love her anymore. I don't think I ever did. I had loved the idea of her; the first girl to ever give me any attention; the first girl that I had ever thought it was possible to be my girlfriend. Do you understand what I mean?"

"Yes, I do." I did understand, but it didn't mean that I liked her talking about how she had loved Danika. But if this is what I had to go through to get the whole story, then so be it.

"Good, because I only want you as my girlfriend," Olivia said seriously, staring at me in the eye. I smiled, telling her that I was okay. Feeling bold at that moment, I leaned over and kissed her on the lips, really reassuring her that it was okay. The peck made a smile form on her pink lips.

162

"So I told her," Olivia said, continuing her story once again. "She rejected me, of course, because she said she wasn't gay, but also because she didn't want her life to change because she wanted to be with a girl."

Olivia's eyes were hard as she spoke. "But this isn't why I don't trust her anymore. I don't trust her because she couldn't just reject me; no, she had to tell the entire school that I was bisexual. Though most people focused on the fact that I like the opposite sex in some shape or form." Olivia stood then crossing her arms over her stomach as if to protect herself. She began pacing as the words spilled out in a rush. I was never a violent person, but at that moment, I really wanted to find Danika and punch her square in the face.

"Everyone thought that I came out by myself. Everyone always said, *Oh she is so brave for coming out all on her own.* I didn't come out because I wanted to! I was forced out," Olivia snarled, almost shouting. I didn't stop her either.

"Danika literally told everybody, and those that she didn't, it traveled to them. I didn't want my parents to hear that their daughter liked girls from somebody else, so I told them. I wanted it to come from me."

"At first, no one accepted me. They shunned me like I was some sickness that they could catch. I was alone then more than ever. I found out that my best friend and the one I thought I loved didn't even want to be near me because she thought that I wanted to cop a feel," Olivia said rolling her eyes, then plopping down next to me. Olivia breathed through her nose, blowing off steam. She was quiet, trying to gather her thoughts. I didn't say anything either, still trying to process what she just told me.

"When people noticed that my parents accepted me the way I was, everyone went back to normal with them kissing up to me, but now for both my looks and my bravery."

"So this is why you don't want me to hang out with Danika?"

Olivia nodded. "Yes, I don't want you to get hurt like I did." I scooted over close to her, wrapping my arm around her waist and buried my head in her shoulder. I wasn't too thrilled that Danika had hurt my Olivia in such a way, but I was happy that we're together.

Somehow, indirectly, our relationship had been all because of Danika. I didn't like it one bit, but if it meant that I was able to get Olivia out of it, then I was okay.

This fact also didn't make me want to punch Danika any less.

CHAPTER 23
Familiar Feelings

The weekend gave me some time to think of what I was going to do about Danika. I don't think I wanted to be associated with her after what I learned about what she did to Olivia. Obviously, she wasn't a very good person if she outed Olivia publicly. I was surprised she hadn't told anyone at school about Olivia and me. At this point, I didn't even care if she tells everyone.

It was strange that I was able to get over Danika harassing me, but what she did to Olivia, I just couldn't stop thinking about it.

I didn't understand why Danika would reject Olivia, and then try to befriend her girlfriend. I wanted to know what Danika was playing at. I did figure out that Danika was only trying to befriend me because of Olivia, which was the easy part.

After a lot of pacing and stuffing my face with gummy bears, I decided that I was going to man up and speak to Danika. Though I was a little frightened to actually confront her, I was going to do it for the sake of Olivia.

When school had ended, I stuffed the things I needed in my backpack then slammed it shut, ready to find Danika. I was going to talk to her earlier that school day, but she was surrounded by her so-called friends. I didn't want to have a talk with Danika with her judgmental friends around. She looked happy, smiling and whatnot. But I knew better.

So I waited till after school when I saw her across the hall, doing the same as me putting her things into her locker, ready to go home. Neither Olivia nor Danika's friends were in sight, so this was the perfect moment.

I let out a breath before walking over to Danika. She looked at me with a light smile before continuing what she was doing. I didn't return the smile. "We n-need to talk." I was trying to sound like I meant business, but I don't think it was working because of my slight stutter.

"Sure. What's up?" Danika said lightly, closing her locker.

I scratched my cheek awkwardly before speaking, "Stop m-messing around with Olivia."

Danika laughed a little bit and put her signature smirk on her face. "Are you serious? What are you talking about?" I crossed my arms over my chest, trying to look as serious as possible.

"I know w-what happened with you and Olivia. I-I want you to stop playing your games."

Danika scoffed with a condescending tone. "I see you talked to Olivia. She probably twisted the story her own way so you can pity her."

"I trust her, I don't trust you. Just back off. Haven't you hurt her enough? Now, you just think you can come back and play nice like nothing happened." I was glad that I didn't stutter once so that my statement would come off as serious.

Danika grimaced a little before speaking, "Did you ever think she might have hurt me?"

My face morphed with confusion. "Why would I think that? I care about Olivia, and you outed her to everybody! It's a no-brainer on why I didn't think about your feelings." I raised my voice a little, and it was strange because I never raised my voice, but now, Olivia was hurting, and it gave me a reason to be upset.

The small number of people left over in the hallway turned to look at us with curious glances. I couldn't care less.

166

I was only focused on the fact that Danika tried to turn this on Olivia. I clutched my hands at my sides; the feeling to punch Danika was coming back.

"Yes, I did. But it wasn't purposely. I had told Cassidy because I thought she would help me sort through everything after Olivia confessed her feelings to me." I flinched again, not liking that Olivia had feelings for someone else at one point.

"Cassidy opened her big mouth and told everyone. I didn't want it to happen, but it did. Then I realized I had feelings for her in return. I told her how I felt but she, of course, rejected me because she had met you."

Though I was still angry at Danika, my heart warmed a little bit at her words. I smiled just a little when I felt a reoccurring tug that has been happening lately in my heart. It was weird, but it felt nice. I had a small urge to rub the spot over my heart.

Though my smile was not for Danika, I was not happy enough to give her any kindness.

"What does this have to do with me though? Why did you harass me then try to be my friend?"

"I don't know. I was trying to force myself to get over her, and what better way to do that than with Olivia's girlfriend. I don't even really understand what she sees in you," Danika said with a sort of envious glare.

Of course, I have thought the same thing plenty of times. Olivia was really out of my league regarding personality and status. It's a real wonder what she saw in me. I had no idea why Olivia would pick me over Danika. I had nothing that Danika has. I really couldn't compare.

"To tell you the truth, I don't know either. Look at me, there is nothing special about me. I'm just normal, and clearly, I don't look like you." I gestured towards Danika's curvy body and then gestured at my almost flat as a board body. "But she obviously saw more than what she saw in you."

My words may have been a little harsh, but it was true.

167

Danika sighed. "You're right. I know when to cut my losses." With a dejected shrug, she turned on her heel. She was about to walk away when she turned back and said: "I know I hurt Olivia; please tell her that I'm sorry."

I nodded. I would tell her.

~

I did tell Olivia about it later that night over the phone. She didn't seem too happy that I had actually gone and spoke to Danika.

"You shouldn't have done that. The whole Danika thing doesn't involve you." Olivia's voice said through the speaker.

Since it was around 11:30, I had already taken a shower and was curled up in my bed under the covers, ready to go to sleep but not before I called Olivia.

"Anything that involves you—involves me," I responded.

Olivia laughed a little bit. "Sometimes, I think you are too good for me."

"I don't know where you got that idea. You are clearly too good for me." This was true in every sense of the word. Sometimes, I didn't think I was enough for her at all.

I heard some movement over the phone. "Are you about to go to bed because I can get off the phone if you like?" I heard some more rustling in the background before Olivia spoke.

"Actually, no. I have a surprise for you." I perked up a little at her words. I really do love surprises.

"What is it?"

"You will see in like two minutes," Olivia answered cryptically. But then again, I do sort of hate surprises. I always can feel the anticipation nagging at the back of my head.

"Ugh, just tell me now. I hate waiting." I groaned, slamming my hand down on my duvet.

"Fine. Come open your window." I sat there for a moment, puzzled then I reacted. I threw my duvet over my body, the cold air hitting me instantly, causing me to shiver. I shuffled my way over the window of my room that was just above the back porch of our house; my only light source being the moonlight streamed through the window.

I can see the faint shape of a person on my backyard lawn. I tried to lift the window, but after a couple of moments, it didn't open. I stared dumbly at the window, wondering if I needed to work out more because obviously, if I couldn't get a window open, something was wrong.

I smacked myself on the forehead when I realized I didn't unlock it first. Sometimes, I wonder if I have a brain at all.

I successfully lifted the window, poking my head out a little so that I could see better. But then I realized I can't see much at all because I left my glasses on the end table.

"One second!" I whisper-shouted to who I could only assume was Olivia. I quickly grabbed my glasses off of the end table. I slipped them on the bridge of my nose then I rushed back over to the window, poking my head out again.

"Having trouble there?" Olivia said with a playful smirk, putting her hand on her hip. I smiled back shyly. Of course, she saw me struggling.

"No, the window was just jammed," I whisper-shouted. I didn't want to make too much noise; if I did, I might wake Gwen and my parents. I didn't want Gwen to know that Olivia was sneaking over to see me, in the middle of the night no less. My father probably wouldn't care as long as I came back safely, and my mother would throw a fit.

"Really?" Olivia retorted, not believing me for a second. She really had no right to, especially after she saw me struggling to lift it.

"Yes, really. What are you doing here?" I said, finally getting around the reason why she was here in the middle of the night.

"I thought you might want to go somewhere with me." Okay, I think Olivia has lost it. It was almost 12 at night, and Olivia wanted to take me somewhere. She had the strangest taste in what she thought was fun.

"Okay, what have you done with my sane girlfriend?" I said with a blank face. Olivia laughed in her hand, trying to be as quiet as possible as well.

"Really, come on. It will be fun, I promise. When have I ever lied?" Olivia asked, putting on the best pouty face she could muster. I'll admit all the surprises Olivia had planned for me had been great, so why should this one be any different. I think my opinion was also being swayed by the insanely adorable pout Olivia was sporting.

"Fine! I give in." I sighed in defeat, knowing my resolve was weak against all things Olivia.

"Yes!" Olivia danced on her toes then exclaimed, "Not that I don't love that onesie that you have on right now, but I need you to hurry up and get dressed."

My face flushed bright red in the darkness as I looked at my duck covered onesies. I forgot I was even wearing it. I regret it on so many levels now.

"Wait there," I said, angling my face away so that she couldn't see my blush. I knew she could see it anyways because Olivia nodded with a light chuckle.

I shut the window quickly and quietly moved around my room to find something to wear. I picked up some simple cargo pants, a V-neck shirt, and a hoodie. I slipped a pair of Converse on before tiptoeing over to the door.

I peeked my head out just a little bit to make sure no one was coming down the hall. When the coast was clear, I trotted quietly down the hall and the stairs. I paused on the last step when I heard a low murmur coming from the living room.

I listened closely, trying to identify the sound. It was the sound of a TV playing.

"Shit," I cursed silently. Of course, my father would watch TV this late on the night I was trying to sneak out. I knew it was my father because he liked to fall asleep on the couch with the infomercials playing in the background.

At least it wasn't my mother, but still, it meant that I wasn't able to sneak out.

I groaned inwardly before making my way back upstairs, to my room, and over to my window, where Olivia was still waiting.

I lifted the window without any trouble this time. "My father is sitting right in the living room. If I try to leave, he will hear me. There is no way for me to come out," I said dejectedly, shoulders sagging.

Olivia smiled nonetheless like I didn't just give her bad news. "That's no problem," she said. "Just climb onto the roof then I'll catch you."

My mouth dropped just a little. Olivia really didn't expect a clumsy girl like me to climb onto a roof then jump down. No way was that ever going to happen.

"I-I can't."

"Stop being a wuss and jump," Olivia said with a playful smile, beckoning me to her with a wave of her hand.

"I-I'll probably break something. I-I can't do it." I shook my head vehemently. I looked over the side of the roof, trying to gauge the distance. It was a far jump, especially onto the hard solid ground. I could definitely break something.

"Not if I catch you," Olivia retorted quickly, having an answer to everything. I shook my head again.

"I still break something, or worse, you will break something."

Olivia smiled up at me with a soft smile. "Do you trust me?"

171

"Yes," I answered without hesitation. Of course, I trusted her. I don't even know why she asked.

"Then jump. I'll catch you, I promise," Olivia said earnestly, trying to make me believe her. Olivia didn't even have to try to convince me. I had no doubt that she would. So I nodded.

I heard Olivia squeal with excitement as I put my leg through the window. I was fairly small, so it was no problem; that was the easy part. The hard part would be getting down.

I was out the window in no time. Now, I was sitting on the roof, staring down at Olivia.

"Now, what?" From where I was sitting, it wasn't as far as I had originally thought, but it still looked pretty high.

"You jump, silly. But try not to slip. Can you do that?" Olivia said with arms reaching for me. Now that I was looking at Olivia, with a large smile stretched over her face, her hair blowing in the wind, and eye trained solely on me, I felt it again.

It was the same feeling I had gotten when I was at the carnival with Olivia for our first date, or when I was talking to Danika earlier.

There was a small tug in my chest followed by a warm sensation. I could feel my heart rate speeding up just a little. These feelings made me want to jump around excitedly or pepper kisses all over Olivia's face.

And that's what I did as soon as I jumped into her arms. Not the jumping around part though.

When my body collided with Olivia's, her legs gave way, and she fell backward into the grass. At first, Olivia coughed a little bit, having the wind knocked out of her.

"Are you okay?" I asked worriedly, cupping her face in my hands. Olivia wheezed before she squeaked out an answer.

"I'm fine. Are you? Nothing is broken right?" I shook my head before kissing the sides of her face then kissing her jaw and finally kissing her lips. I didn't realize how much I missed her till our lips connected and I felt her hands rest on my hips.

172

Olivia automatically let me deepen the kiss, though we were still lying in the grass. We lay there for a moment, lazily kissing each other until Olivia spoke.

"No matter how much I like making out in the grass, it's making me all itchy," she said with a laugh. I climbed off her, standing up straight then reaching out to pull her up with me.

"Where to now?"

"I'll show you." Olivia reached out, grabbing my hand and began walking to the front of my house.

"Where is your car?" I asked, noticing that the vehicle was nowhere in sight.

"I thought it would be okay if we walked. It's not far from here and its really nice out." I had to agree with her, it was really nice out. The temperature was just right, so it wasn't too hot or too cold. There were plenty of stars out shining bright, along with a crescent moon.

"I don't mind," I said truthfully because I really didn't. We walked in silence for a while, contented with just having our joined hands sway between us. I broke the silence when I thought of something Danika had said earlier. I didn't want to be thinking of Danika right now, but I couldn't help it, what she said bothered me a little.

"Olivia?"

"Yes?" she said absentmindedly as she looked at the houses we passed by.

"Why do you like me?" Olivia looked at me curiously when I spoke. She didn't speak, Olivia just stared at me. I assumed she was thinking about it. I hoped I didn't come off as insecure.

"Well," Olivia started. "You're simple. As in you know what you like and you know what you don't. Though you're a little scared of what other people may think of you, you try to lay your feelings on the table. Your honest, funny, kind, and let's not forget just plain adorable. How could I not like you?"

I shrugged, not knowing the answer to her rhetorical question. "I don't know. I just think sometimes that I am not good enough for you, that you could be better off with someone else."

"I'm better off with you," Olivia responded. I pulled her close, wrapping my arm around her waist. She automatically put her arm on my shoulder and kissed me on the forehead.

"Okay, one more question just because I'm nosy."

"Shoot."

"When did you realize that you liked me?" Olivia shook with light laughter. She looked at me with mirth in her brown eyes.

"I would say as soon as I saw you at the carnival, but to be honest, when we were sitting on the hill that one time and you blurted out 'Do you want a sucker?', I was a goner after that." I flushed in embarrassment. I had such a way with words.

"Although you did look pretty hot with a busted nose." I pushed her away a little bit with my hip as we both laughed, remembering the incident.

Her laugh brings back the tug in my chest. I don't know what it was, the familiar feeling that I got whenever I was around Olivia. It was something that I had surely never felt before. It was a new feeling that I could only associate with Olivia.

I knew I would soon find out what this familiar feeling was and what it all meant. But for now, I would just be happy with being with Olivia.

CHAPTER 24
Compelled To Do What We Have Been Forbidden

Okay, so where Olivia was taking me turned out to be not that exciting. Well, for me anyways. She thought it would be fun to go night swimming in the country club's pool. I don't know where Olivia got the idea.

That's why she came over in the middle of the night, then made me jump from a roof just so she could go night swimming.

I wasn't a fan of swimming in the first place, but I guess if Olivia was here with me it could be fun. I was really curious to see how we would actually get in the place when the gate that led to the pool, without having to go through the main country club lobby, was locked.

"So what's your plan to get us in?" I said feeling a little smug that this seemed to be the only thing she didn't think through. But it was short-lived when she pulled a key from her pocket.

"I'm friends with the guy who cleans the pool," Olivia answered while sticking the key in the lock. The lock came off easily without any trouble.

"Of course you are. Are we even allowed in here?" Though she had the key, I was still a little worried that we were not supposed to be here. I was pretty sure we weren't.

Olivia held open the gate, allowing me to walk in first then she followed behind me. "Uh that's the tricky part, no we're not." I gawked at her for a short moment, and she stared back, waiting for my reaction. Then without a word, I walked toward to gate to leave. Before I could even get out the gate, Olivia grabbed my arm, pulling me back.

"Come on, we're already here. Mind as well have fun," Olivia begged.

"T-This is illegal!"

"Yeah, but we're already here. It's too late, you're an accessory to trespassing," Olivia said with a sweet smile, flashing her pearly whites, trying to look innocent. The reason she didn't tell me where we were going was that she knew I would refuse to be involved in something that was illegal.

I still shook my head. I swear Olivia loves to drag me out of my comfort zone. Sometimes, it does seem to be a good thing because before, I would never even dream of breaking into a pool area with a beautiful girl that I was able to call my girlfriend. Boy have things changed.

"Come on, please?" Olivia whined once more just for good measure because I was pretty sure she already knew I was going to give in. Can anyone say whipped?

My willpower was useless around Olivia. Once again, I nodded. Olivia squealed then pecked me on the lips. I smiled at her with a lopsided grin. I guess it was worth it.

But what can I say; people do crazy things when they're in love.

Holy shit. Did I just say that? I wasn't in love with Olivia, at least I don't think. But I mean how would I know, I have never been in love before. I didn't even know what love was.

My eyes widened as I looked at Olivia. My tendency to go along with all of Olivia nefarious plots would say otherwise. Also the fact that I can't seem to not think about her when she wasn't there or the feelings I felt when she was around.

"Joey? You okay?" Olivia asked, staring at me with worried eyes. I hadn't even noticed that I spaced out for a

176

second. I almost spaced out again when I looked into Olivia's brown eyes.

A dopey smile appeared on my face again. I think I might actually be in love. "I'm great."

"Good. You had me worried there for a second. Let's swim!" Olivia squealed, pulling me over to the edge of the sparkling blue pool. Lights illuminated under the water, making the water look almost like crystals.

Olivia bent down, trailing her hands in the water to feel for temperature. The blue light fell over her frame in waves, making her skin appear the same beautiful turquoise color of the water.

It really was the perfect moment for me to push Olivia into the water, but I wanted her to stay that way just a little longer.

Olivia stood up once again, the color of the pool never moving from her face. Olivia smiled at me, and I smiled back.

I pulled off my shoes and my hoodie as Olivia pulled off hers. I tossed them to the side then I realized something. "I didn't bring a swimsuit," I said, scratching my head dumbly.

"Okay, you caught me," Olivia said, putting her hands up in surrender, then her features turned suggestive. "I just wanted to see you in your underwear." Olivia trailed her finger down my abdomen. I almost gave into her for a second; I could feel myself leaning in.

But the urge came back to push her in, so I did. Her surprised face was comical as she hit the water. I burst out laughing. I laughed so hard, I started to clutched my stomach because it began to hurt.

Then I realized that Olivia hadn't resurfaced. I stopped laughing immediately and began to search the water for Olivia. I felt my heart actually stop beating when I didn't see her.

"Olivia?" I called out. I got apprehensive when I didn't get a response.

Then Olivia popped out of the water near the edge grabbing onto my ankles. "Gotcha!" she screamed. I was so scared that I slipped on some water that was splashed on the tile when Olivia fell. I tittered right over the edge of the pool then fell in.

When I resurfaced, I pushed my now wet blonde hair out of my face. Olivia floated next to me with a huge grin on her face.

"I was going to pull you in, but you managed to slip in all by yourself," Olivia said, laughing about as hard as I was. I splashed water on her face, but she still giggled.

I pulled her by the soggy shirt to me, trying to pull her in for a kiss, but she smoothly turned away, and my lips landed on her damp cheek.

"Nope, you don't get a kiss. That was really mean." Olivia pouted, even though what she did to me was also mean. The water began to seem a little colder as she struggled a little in my grasp. I started to shiver slightly.

"N-Now who is being the cockblock?" Olivia just smirked playfully at me, noticing me shiver. "What you did to me was mean. I could have slipped and fell and hit my head on the tile rather than fell in the pool."

Olivia put her arm around my waist the paddled her way over to the wall where she propped herself against it and pulled me to her. Olivia pecked me lightly on the lips before whispering. "Okay, I'm sorry."

"I'm sorry too," I whispered back, leaning forward to kiss her. Her lips were warm compared to the cool temperature of the water. I smiled a little into the kiss when I tasted chlorine for the pool on Olivia's lips. Olivia deepened the kiss by sliding her tongue through my parted lips, and I reacted by running my hands in her now damp locks. We stayed kissing each other for a while. I honestly lost track of time.

We were finally forced apart when a beam of light began to flash in our faces. "Get out of the pool!" A voice shouted timidly. My eyes widened and so did Olivia's when we heard the voice.

We split apart immediately. Olivia hoisted herself out of the pool first then she reached out to help me, since I didn't have much upper body strength.

I knew we were in trouble when I looked in the face of the person who spoke. The security guard seemed to be in his mid-twenties. His face was flushed in the light of his flashlight, but he still looked a little angry.

So Olivia and I stood, huddled cold in our dripping wet clothing. Olivia opened her mouth to speak, but the man cut her off. "Don't even try to tell some lie because I'm smart enough to know what was going on here."

We stood in cold silence, knowing when not to speak. Then I felt an anger flare through me when I noticed the security guard's eyes trailing up Olivia's body. Of course, her light pink shirt would be seen through once wet.

I glared at the man before stalking, more like sloshing over to where we tossed our things. I grabbed up our things and walked back to them. I draped my hoodie over Olivia's frame, which she wrapped it around herself.

"You were saying?" I snapped at the man.

He cleared his throat and looked at us. We were a pitiful sight; both of us looking like drowned rats.

"Look, I won't call the police, which I should because you are trespassing. I was a teenager once too." The guard said, with a little reminiscent glint in his eye. "But I do have to escort you home and notify your parents what has happened tonight."

And just when I thought I was in the clear, he said that. Let's just hope my mom doesn't answer the door.

~

Obviously, luck was not on my side that night because after the guard dropped Olivia off at her home and drove me to mine, my mother opened the door when the guard knocked.

On the outside, she looked calm and collected, but I knew from the look in her eye that she was furious.

After the guard calmly explained to her that we were found in the country club pool, minus the making out part, she escorted him out the door with a friendly smile. As soon as the door closed, her smile was gone.

A thick silence filled the space within the foyer. My mother didn't speak; she just stood there with her mouth in a thin line. I stood near the stairs, staring back at her, not wanting to be the one that speaks or moves first.

"What were you thinking?" I flinched at first, a little surprised at the volume of her voice. I opened my mouth to speak, but she cut me off. "No, don't answer that. You weren't thinking!"

My mother scoffed in anger then pinched the bridge of her nose. "I thought she would be good for you to help you clean up your act, but no. Instead, you two are screwing around."

"It's not like that," I said softly, trying to defend ourselves.

"Then what is it like? Hmm? I'm not stupid. I see how you and that little slut of a lesbian look at each other!" My mother growled at me taking steps toward me. I didn't move. I stood my ground staring her in the eye.

"Don't call her that."

"I will call her whatever I please!" Apparently, my mother was louder than I thought because Gwen came stumbling sleepily down the stairs, rubbing her eyes.

"What is going on? Why are you all wet?" Gwen said in a hoarse voice, her eyes on me. She didn't even realize the tension going on between my mother and me.

"Oh, I'll tell you why she is all wet." My mother sneered, backing away from me only to pace. "She snuck out in the middle of the night to go swimming with Olivia Winchester."

180

Gwen shrugged and yawned a bit in her hand. "What's the big deal? It's not like she got put in jail."

My mother whipped around to Gwen, staring at her with cold eyes. "You knew about them being together?" She hissed. While I flinched again at her tone, Gwen stood calm and collected.

"Yes, I knew."

"You knew, and you did not tell me."

"Yeah, I didn't think it was a big deal if they were in a relationship or not." Gwen leaned on the railing, looking bored and tried. The whole conversation didn't seem to bother her at all, but I was just waiting for my mother to explode.

"Oh, it's a big deal. In this world, it's all about reputation. And having a daughter like that," My mother pointed her finger at me. "Already puts me at the bottom of the barrel. Now, what do you think will happen when they find out that my failure of a daughter is gay!"

I could feel my throat tighten which was usually a sign that I was going to cry. It hurt me to know that my mother thought about me that way. Usually, I put it to the back of my mind. But now she is in front of me saying that I am a failure and that she won't accept me the way that I am, it hurts more than ever.

"Nothing is wrong with her!" Gwen shouted, no longer tired or bored. "If Jo is gay or not, she is still my sister and still your daughter. If other people can't accept her the way she is, then screw them."

My mother looked surprised that Gwen would come to my defense. I wasn't surprised at all. Gwen was my sister, and I knew she cared for me.

Where is my father during all of this you may ask? Well, he is probably out like a log in his room or not even home.

"Olivia is openly gay, and everyone still accepts her." Gwen pointed out.

My mother sneered. "Olivia is charming, beautiful, and popular. That's all anyone cares about. I cannot have a daughter who is gay. If the Winchesters allow their child to be gay, so be it."

I have had enough. I have been quiet this whole time, but every time my mother opened her mouth, I could feel something bubbling up inside of me. Who was she to decide who I was to be and who I should be with? I couldn't take her badmouthing anymore.

"What makes this about you at all?" I said softly, staring at the floor. My mother looked away from Gwen and narrowed her eyes at me.

"What?" she said in a low voice. I looked up from the ground and stared at her head on.

"This isn't about you. Somehow, you always make everything about yourself when it isn't." I started off calm, but then I can feel the anger inside me surfacing. "This is my life! Not yours! I will date whoever I want!"

"You are under my roof, so your life involves me. When my reputation lies on who you date, it involves me! I will say who you can and cannot date, and you most certainly will not date that harlot!"

I stepped up to my mother, standing up straight as possible. My mother could talk bad about me all she wanted, but she will not insult Olivia. "You don't know her! You will not badmouth her, especially not when I am here to say something about."

"You will not speak to me that way." I could see a fire light in my mother's eyes. In my opinion, she was taking this way too far, but I was not about to back down. I looked at Gwen for support. She looked almost proud. It was all I needed to continue.

"You will not speak about Olivia that way. I will date Olivia! Screw your damn reputation!"

182

Suddenly, my mother's hand struck my cheek. I could hear Gwen gasp from where she was standing on the stairs, but all I could focus on was the throbbing sensation on my cheek.

"Mother!" Gwen shouted, trotting down the stairs to me. Though my cheek was stinging in pain and I knew it was turning red, I turned my head back to my mother and stared her in the eye.

"I'm in love with her."

Silence fell upon us, even Gwen stopped her movements toward me. I had finally admitted it, and I didn't regret it at all. I could feel that I really did love her. I loved Olivia.

If my cheek wasn't hurting like a bitch right now, I might have smiled. Also, I think this really wasn't the time for me to be smiling like a lovesick fool.

Then an idea seemed to spark in my mother's eyes. I think Gwen saw it too because she stood in front of me in defense. We didn't know what my mother was about to say or do, but we both knew it wouldn't be a good thing.

My mother looked smug like she just came up with the greatest idea yet. "You know what, I had enough. I'm sure your grandmother will be happy to care for the likes of you."

Gwen gasps as she realizes what my mother meant. I still was focused on the fuzzy feeling I felt in my chest, so I wasn't really paying attention. "Mother, don't."

"No, Gwen! This is what this family needs!" My mother bellowed. This caught my attention. She wouldn't, at least I thought she wouldn't. "This family doesn't need you here anymore. You will live with your grandmother from here on out." My mother finished with a snake-like smile. She crossed her arms over her chest, feeling really smug.

I felt my world imploding then and there. I couldn't feel, I couldn't think, I couldn't breathe. My mother wanted to send me away. I would be apart from Olivia. If she were to send me away, I would no longer be able to spend countless hours just being with Olivia. Olivia could no longer surprise me with dates and take me to places that I wouldn't usually go. I wouldn't have Neal to goof off when things got stressful or a Gwen to support me through thick or thin.

I wouldn't be able to hold Olivia's hand in mine. I wouldn't be able to kiss Olivia's lips. I wouldn't be able to tell Olivia I loved her every second of every day.

My throat tightened, and my eyes welled up with tears. "Y-You can't do this." My voice cracked.

"I can, and I will." Gwen looked about as torn up as I felt. Gwen opened her mouth to speak, but I spoke first; louder this time.

"You can't do this!" My whole body was shaking, and tears ran quickly down my face. "The one time I'm happy, you take it away from me!"

"I don't care about your happiness." My mother snarled. Gwen stood in front of me and began to combat my mother's decision. They went back and forth.

But I couldn't stand it anymore, so I ran. I ran out the door and straight to Olivia's.

CHAPTER 25
You're the One That I Love

Tears had stopped streaming down my face when I arrived at Olivia's house, but in its place, my lungs began to burn. I should I have felt exhausted as I climbed the steps and stood on the porch, yet I didn't. The only thing that was on my mind was Olivia.

I raised my hand to the door but hesitated when I realized that it was late at night. I might wake Olivia's parents. But I knocked anyway. I had to see Olivia.

A few seconds later, when no one answered, I knocked again; harder this time.

Finally, I heard shuffling on the other side of the door. I bounced on my toes impatiently, hoping it was Olivia.

It was Olivia who opened the door. She looked thoroughly surprised when she saw me standing there. I mean who wouldn't be when someone showed up at your door this late at night.

She was dressed in some yoga shorts and a tank top with a robe over it. If the sight of her didn't make tears well up in my eyes all over again, I most likely would have stared at her toned legs, but my vision was blurred.

"Joey, what's wrong?" Olivia said, rushing forward to envelop me in a hug, putting her arms around my waist. I returned the hug, wrapping my arms around the mid-section of her back, our bodies fitting together like two puzzle pieces. I buried my head in her shoulder, crying a little harder when I was hit with the smell of lilacs and mint.

185

"Come on, let's go inside." Olivia then shuffled with me in tow into her living room. She sat us down on the couch. The tears just wouldn't stop coming, especially now that I was here in Olivia's arms and she was rubbing my back in soothing circles.

Olivia didn't even pester me about what was wrong, she just let me cry. I don't even remember the last time I cried this much. When I finally stopped, I wiped my face with my hands.

"I'm sorry. I got your shirt all wet," I commented, noticing the wet spot on her shoulder. Olivia wiped the spot absentmindedly.

"No problem. I'm just worried about you. What happened?"

"My mother happened." Worry was evident in Olivia's brown eyes as she stared at me, waiting for me to continue.

"My mother lost it when she found out that you and I were in a relationship and that we were out night swimming. She even slapped me when I said I was going to date you no matter what." Olivia's hands flew up to my face, cradling it softly.

Her eyes narrowed as she examined my face. "That bitch," she whispered. Even with me knowing everything that I had to say to Olivia, I couldn't help but crack a smile and laugh a bit.

"Yes, I know," I said, still smiling, but then my smile fell. "But that's not even the worst part."

Olivia noticed the tone of my voice because she pulled her eyes away from my face and looked into my eyes instead.

"What?"

I took a deep breath, closing my eyes and leaning into Olivia's touch. When I opened them, Olivia was still staring at me, waiting for what I had to say. "My mother...my mother wants to send me away to live with my grandmother."

Olivia didn't say anything. She just blinked a coupled times with her mouth gaping open. "She can't."

186

"But she will." Olivia shook her head back and forth, clearly not believing what I had just said. I fell back into her, wrapping my arms around her waist and burying my face into her shoulder once more. Olivia closed her eyes and laid her hand on top of mine.

"It's is partly my fault. She probably wouldn't even bring it up if I hadn't said…" I trailed off. I didn't think this was the right moment for me to tell Olivia that I was in love with her. I would prefer a more romantic setting.

Not with Olivia sitting in her PJs, face stoic, along with me with a tear-stained face and still in the damp clothes that I had gone swimming in.

"Had said what?" Of course, she would pry when I didn't want to tell her. I sat up slightly, feeling this was a moment where I should be looking at Olivia. She looked back at me with a curious gaze.

"If I hadn't said that I was in love with you." Olivia was silent. She just stared at me, brown eyes swirling with emotion after emotion. I waited patiently, bouncing my knee with nervousness.

When minutes passed, and Olivia still didn't say a word, I spoke. "L-Look, it's just I wanted you to know how I feel, especially before I have to leave. I…I don't expect you to say it—" Olivia cut me off by putting her lips to mine. It was short but soft and slow, but it made my heart beat wildly.

When we parted, Olivia said, "I love you too." A grin broke out over my face, and my heart increased in speed. I couldn't believe that Olivia loved me back; it really felt all too surreal. "You have to know that."

I pecked her on the lips. "I know that now." I was glad that I did. The spell between us broke suddenly, and Olivia stood up quickly, putting her hands on her head.

"She can't take you away from me." I sat there only the couch feeling useless. Olivia let out a slow breath, and then she put her hand out to me. "Come on, let's get some sleep." I didn't even realize how tired I actually was until she mentioned it. I nodded, taking her hand.

~

I always knew my mother was something else with planning, but this was ridiculous.

By the time I woke up in Olivia's bed, went downstairs and ate breakfast with Olivia's family, then dragged my body back to the hellhole that I called home, my mother had called my grandmother and told her what was going on as well as booked me on the first flight out of there.

I couldn't believe it; I almost burst into tears all over again.

I sat on my bed with my knees tucked in and my head bowed between them. I didn't even want to start packing. If I did, it would make it all real. My flight wasn't until later that day, so I had time to sulk around.

I could hear footsteps coming toward me, but I didn't lift my head. From the audible clicks on the wooden floor, I could tell it was my mother's heels.

"You need to start packing." I still didn't look up, not caring to look at my mother's face right now. My mother snapped her fingers angrily to get my attention. Of course, I looked up. "Look at me when I'm speaking. You're not going to miss your flight." With that, she walked out, not saying another word.

Gwen came in shortly after, with Neal following behind her. I automatically got up and ran to him. Neal wrapped his arms around me in a tight hug. "It will be okay."

"But I won't be," I said pulling away and wiping my face after I let a few tears escape. I sure would miss his scrawny frame and unruly red hair.

"I'll help you pack." Gwen supplied with a somber look. I nodded, not really caring if I packed or not. I slumped on the bed again. Neal sat beside me, putting an arm around my shoulder.

"What am I going to do? I won't be able to hang out with you anymore or see Olivia."

"We will find a way. I promise," Neal said, trying to be comforting. But nothing could make me feel better at that moment.

Neal pulled something from his jacket pocket with a sad smile. "Look, I brought you some gummy bears. For old times' sake." I smiled back, taking the bag and ripping it open then pouring some in Neal's open hands.

"I don't even know where she got the idea to send you away. It's not even a big deal that you are in a relationship with Olivia." Gwen huffed, carrying a suitcase in her hand that she pulled from my closet. She started throwing things randomly into the bag, in a frustrated manner.

I shrugged, not having the answer either. So we sat there, packing my clothes. Really, it was Gwen packing my things while Neal and I tossed gummy bears into the air trying to catch them with our mouths. After a while, Gwen even joined in as well.

As the hours passed, our time together became bittersweet because I knew I would be leaving Gwen and Neal.

Finally, I was done packing whatever I could fit into two large suitcases. The rest, Gwen promised to send to me. I made sure to grab some of the photos of Olivia and me that we had taken, along with pictures of Gwen and Neal. The rest of the pictures would stay tacked on my walls.

As Neal struggled to get one of the suitcases down the stairs, I realized that I had forgotten something important.

I left the suitcase in the hall and rushed back to my room. I went over to my desk, opening the drawer that held Olivia's pink jacket. I pulled it out carefully as if it might shatter. I stared at it for a moment, remembering when Olivia gave it to me.

I ran my hands over the white letters on that back that spelled Olivia's last name. I slipped it on, pulling it around me. I

189

smiled a little when it covered my hands at the end of the sleeves.

"Josephine! Come on, or you will be late!" My mother shouted from the foyer. I didn't even bother to respond; I just dragged my feet into the hall and began lugging the suitcase down the steps.

"Where's Olivia?" I said directing my question at Gwen when I reached the bottom of the stairs. My mother scoffed, motioning for Neal to take my suitcase. He took it from my hands then made it out to the car.

"She texted me that she will be here in a few minutes," Gwen answered, ignoring my mother's annoyed glare. I nodded then headed over to the porch, where I sat on the stairs to wait for her.

My mother trailed after me. "You will not wear that jacket to the airport."

I whipped around to glare at her. "I will wear whatever I feel like wearing."

Just as my mother was about to speak, my father's car pulled up in the driveway. When it was put into park, Olivia hopped out of the passenger's seat and ran over to me, pulling me into a hug. I was surprised because Olivia was supposed to drive over her by herself and my father was supposed to be at work.

My father calmly got out of the car, still dressed in his work shrubs. He pointed to the bags that were up against the car. "Take your bags back into the house." Everyone looked a little confused at that moment, not understanding what was going on. Everyone stayed in their place.

"Honey, I thought you were at work?" My mother said in a slightly whiney and annoyed tone.

"I was until I realized this was a big mistake."

My mother's mouth gaped open, not understanding what he meant like the rest of us. Was my father going against what my mother wanted?

190

"But Hal, our family doesn't need this insolent child around any longer. Look at her," she said motioning to me and Olivia, who had her arm wrapped around my waist.

"That is our daughter that you are talking about!" My father shouted at my mother. I was thoroughly surprised at his actions. He never went against my mother. But I was glad that he chose this moment to.

"Our daughter wouldn't disobey me the way she does!" My mother bellowed, crossing her arms across her chest.

My father sighed, holding the bridge of his nose with his fingers. Then he looked at my mother with a determined stare. "You have to stop this. You have to let her be who she is. I know that I'm not around often, but I am around enough to know that this person standing here is the daughter I know, not the girl you try her to become."

Olivia took that moment to speak, "Mrs. Montgomery," My mother glared at Olivia when she heard her voice. I held Olivia's hand urging, her to continue. "I know that I'm not what you want for your daughter but...I love her. Shouldn't that be the only thing that matters?" I grinned, my heart warmed at my father's and Olivia's words.

"You don't get to speak to me!" My mother shouted. I automatically stood in front of Olivia, scowling at my mother, about to defend Olivia.

"No, Melody. Don't speak to her that way. Joey stays here. You can't cast her away for being who she is." My mother looked at me, still with some resentment, but also with a small amount of understanding.

"Fine. Let her stay." My mother shook her head then went into the house. All of us stood in silence, staring at the door where my mother just went in. Then my father grinned and came over to me. He kissed me on the forehead and patted Olivia on her head. Soon after, he trotted into the house after my mother.

191

Gwen, Neal, Olivia, and I stood around, not moving. Everything happened so quickly, it hadn't dawned on us yet that I was staying. My father talked my mother into letting me stay. I would be able to stay here with Gwen and Neal, but most importantly, stay here with Olivia.

"Well, that was anticlimactic," Neal said with a large grin. Gwen shoved him with a grin matching his. "What? I really thought she was leaving for a second. It was about to get all dramatic with tears and everything."

Gwen sighed happily then hugged me tightly. With a smile, she said, "Glad it didn't come to that." I wasn't able to speak, still in shock. Neal came over then and gave me a hug and a smile.

"Your mom got her ass handed to her," he said with a laugh. This time I shoved Neal away from me. Having enough of Neal, Gwen dragged him into the house by his ear.

He gave us a thumbs-up before whining, "Ouch!"

Olivia and I were the only ones left outside now. She looked at me with happiness written all over her face. I was sure I looked the same way.

I squealed happily, which was something I never did, and then jumped on Olivia, hugging her tightly. She laughed and spun me around. We probably looked like complete fools, but we didn't care. We only cared that we would be with each other for another day.

When Olivia finally stopped spinning me, she put her lips to mine. I held the sides of her face, holding her in place. I smiled into the kiss, not wanting to break apart for a moment. But eventually, we did since breathing was a necessity.

I knew then that the only thing that matters was her. Everything would be alright as long as Olivia was here with me.

"I love you, Josephine Montgomery," Olivia whispered, pressing her forehead against mine. I smiled, as her brown eyes shone with love.

"And I love you, Olivia Winchester."

192

BOOK YOU MIGHT ENJOY

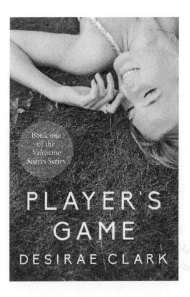

PLAYER'S GAME
Desirae Clark

And when I turned around, I expected to see my annoying little sisters but was instead greeted by a familiar face. In the threshold stood Parker Brady with a devious smirk on his face and the looks of a god.

Samantha Valentine's life turns upside down when she finds out her family is returning to her old town, Scottsdale. It took her a while to make the city her home, and now all of that is for naught, as she has to learn to settle in a quiet town again.

Parker Brady is perfectly happy to make a mess of his life after his best friend, Samantha, left him. He felt betrayed by his most trusted friend, and now he doesn't care about anyone anymore. The only thing that matters to him is getting girls.

The two are not so thrilled when they meet after years of being away. Old grudges resurface from the past.

Will Samantha and Parker restore their broken friendship? Or will something else rise from its ruins?

Player's Game is a funny and heartwarming story about young adults learning to come into terms with their past. If you're up for a light read that will leave you smiling, grab your copy now!

BOOK YOU MIGHT ENJOY

OUTCASTS
BD Fresquez

How can he act so calm and collected after he just stole my first kiss?

Riley Summers doesn't quite fit in the Fairfield High crowd. She listens to Led Zepplin and watches Star Wars—not your usual teenage girl favorites.

She has been fine with living in the fringes of her high school scene until Aiden Callaway, Fairfield's infamous rebel hunk, "kidnaps" her one afternoon. He eventually lets her go, but their time together is far from over.

Join Riley and Aiden on their senior year journey—a year of Star Wars movie marathons, a crashed wedding, a paint war, and something unexpected: a keen, growing attraction.

This might be your next favorite rebel-boy-and-nerd-girl romance. Grab your copy now!

ACKNOWLEDGEMENTS

This was a book that I had no idea that I was going to write until I had a dream, sat down at my computer, and started writing. I don't even remember now what possessed me to post each chapter on Wattpad either. But I'm so glad that I did.

This book has been a life changer for me, and to my surprise, so many others. When I posted on Wattpad for the first time, you couldn't have told me then that it would be as popular as it is now, let alone that it would be getting published. I would have thought you to be insane. Thanks so much to my agent, AJ, and my editor, Winnie, for putting up with my work throughout this! But also all the people at BLVNP, who took a chance on me and working on my book.

First, I want to thank the members of my family. I want to thank my Granny Ma, Lark, and Stacie for taking care of me when I needed them the most. To my siblings, best older sister, Chelsea, and the best twin brother I could ever ask for, Corey. I thank my pseudo siblings, Michaela, for writing random stories when we were kids and Michael, who is always there to listen to me rant about anything and everything. I'm going to thank my nephew Shawn, who can't read right now, for bringing so much happiness to my life that I didn't know I wanted. As well as my grandmother who took me in when I needed her. To my cousin Leon, who holds the best conversation with me but is always quiet when I write. To my dog Teddie, who has been here for everything. And to my parents, who inspired me from such a young age that I could create anything if I wanted to.

Second, to my best friends who have put up with me through all these years. To Cat, who has been putting up with listening to my writer's stress and my complaining, plotting, and whatever else you had to deal with that came with being my best friend since middle school. To Louis, who always has such perfect timing and somehow knows when I'm stressed and takes me out on random movie and dinner dates. To Domonique, who never fails to surprise me with random gifs and memes about books that never fail to make me laugh. And to Shadow who has listened to me think out loud about new ideas for my new books and everything else that I rant about daily.

Lastly to my Wattpad readers, every single one of you. You guys are what made this happen. I have loved every single comment and private message that I have gotten over the years about *Kissing Olivia Winchester*. No community has made me feel that I belong as much as you guys have. I figured out who I am and what I'm supposed to do with my life because of you guys. I could never thank you guys enough. I want you guys to always remember that just like Joey, we all struggle with things that make us different and set us apart, but as long as we stay ourselves, everything else will follow. So stay true to yourselves, keep moving forward, and you will be fine.

AUTHOR'S NOTE

Thank you so much for reading *Kissing Olivia Winchester*! I can't express how grateful I am for reading something that was once just a thought inside my head.

Please feel free to send me an email. Just know that my publisher filters these emails. Good news is always welcome.
athena_simone@awesomeauthors.org

Sign up for my blog for updates and freebies!
athena-simone.awesomeauthors.org

One last thing: I'd love to hear your thoughts on the book. Please leave a review on Amazon or Goodreads because I just love reading your comments and getting to know you!

Can't wait to hear from you!

Athena Simone

ABOUT THE AUTHOR

Athena Simone has always loved to read both fantasy and young adult books, from which she got her inspiration to become a writer. Athena loves a good romance fantasy book which she is happy with just reading for hours on end. She has been writing in secret since middle school until 2013 when she uploaded her first book, *Kissing Olivia Winchester*, on Wattpad. She also has a major in Media Art and Studies and a minor in English. She is the type that is always listening to music, from which she gets a lot of her inspiration to write from.

Made in the USA
Monee, IL
07 May 2020